Recollections
of the
Golden Triangle

OTHER WORKS BY ALAIN ROBBE-GRILLET

Published by Grove Press

Djinn
Topology of a Phantom City
Project for a Revolution in New York
La Maison de Rendez-vous
For a New Novel: Essays on Fiction
Last Year at Marienbad
In the Labyrinth
Jealousy
The Voyeur
The Erasers

Recollections of the Golden Triangle

ALAIN ROBBE-GRILLET

TRANSLATED FROM THE FRENCH BY
J.A. UNDERWOOD

Grove Press, Inc., New York

First published in Great Britain 1984 by John Calder
(Publishers) Ltd, London

Originally published in French, 1978, under the title
Souvenirs du triangle d'or by Les Editions de Minuit, Paris

First Grove Press Edition 1986
First Printing 1986
ISBN: 0-394-55564-3
Library of Congress Catalog Card Number: 86-45233

First Evergreen Edition 1986
First Printing 1986
ISBN: 0-394-62275-8
Library of Congress Catalog Card Number: 86-45233

Printed in the United States of America

Grove Press, Inc., 196 West Houston Street
New York, N.Y. 10014

5   4   3   2   1

Recollections
of the
Golden Triangle

An impression, already, that things are getting narrower. Don't puzzle too much. Don't turn round. Don't stop. Don't force the pace. For no visible reason, no reason. Speed has become necessary. The imminent discovery of the "temple" by the security forces means that the overall plan has to be modified and above all hurried into execution. But without changing anything—it's too late—of the elements that make it up, and that are now inevitable.

There is nothing exceptional about the entrance to the building from the street: a black-painted door of medium size, in other words neither smaller nor larger than its neighbours, with restrained mouldings in Directoire style. It appears to be made of wood, like the others. Its only distinguishing detail, though one doesn't notice this at first, is the complete absence of any handle, keyhole, latch, knocker, bell, etc. There is no guessing whether it opens to the right or to the left. Come to that, it might not even be a door. Avoid this course; it leads nowhere.

The stone surround—pilasters with vertical fluting—is topped by a triangular pediment in the classical style enclosing a second, equilateral triangle standing point downwards and touching the sides of the first with all three vertices. An eye, carved in bas-relief, occupies the centre; but instead of lying horizontally, as in nature and in the manner normally adopted for this type of symbol, the gap between the eyelids here forms a vertical spindle marking the axis of symmetry of the overall design. The hole representing the pupil is pierced so deeply that there is no telling how far in it goes, possibly because of the height at which it is situated in relation to normal eye level.

People will doubtless have realized already, alas, that the door is operated by means of an electronic signal emitted by a small portable device that must be applied to a specific point on the lower panel, etc. (No ratiocinations, no regrets, no going back.) The stone eye serves no purpose, at least not as things stand.

This is where the story starts, after an interruption, probably, a fairly major one giving the impression that things are getting even narrower: just the opposite of an opening. The system as a whole remains, for the moment, strictly motionless.

Motionless again, yes, probably, but with something temporary, brittle, an element of tension, as if over all this calm there reigned, invisible as yet, a threat, a fear, a death sentence already pronounced, still silent, yes, no doubt, but with an almost indiscernible breathing, or whistling as of a wind that, without appearing to be of any force, nevertheless shifts the grains of sand on the beach one by one, carrying them imperceptibly towards the abandoned terrace where, bit by bit, they build up in sinuous little parallel ridges on the gappy grey planks that here blend without a break into the very slight slope of powdery, uneven ground moulded by the treading of innumerable feet the day before, or over the past few days, down to the water, now slack once more, yes, probably, but still breaking at high tide in a tiny wave endlessly repeating itself with a gentle, periodic hiss of such regularity that one might not hear this either, so integral a part is it of this scene caught by the dawn, as one might also fail to be aware of the laboured, soundless flight of a large, pale-coloured pelican moving away to the left, skimming the water about ten metres out, roughly parallel to where the water's edge is marked by a festoon of foam that no sooner vanishes than it is brought back by the inexhaustible and, in any case, from where I am, invisible wavelet, it being too far off, too low down, too much in the background.

Facing me, which is to say coming towards me in the opposite direction to that in which the big bird disappeared, the noticeably livelier silhouette now tracing its arabesques soon turns out to be that of a naked girl mounted bareback on a colt with a flowing mane in the manner currently in vogue among kids on the west coast; advancing erratically, following a capricious course that means they can be admired from every angle in turn and at closer and closer quarters, her long, blue-black hair and the horse's streaming mane and tail like licks of golden flame whirl and gambol in the warm morning breeze as the girl tries without stirrups or spurs to make her pale-brown mount venture farther into the sea, which is splashed up on all sides by its restive hoofs, falling back amid the tinkling laughter of the amazon whose slender, spume-flecked body gleams with a metallic lustre, suddenly, lit by the rising sun.

Having almost reached the foreground, the young rider smelling of iodine and salt in turn disappears to the right behind me, my little bride of the moment; and I do not look round to follow her with my gaze. I even fade further into the indistinct background of scattered tables and stacked chairs in the corner of the terrace when I spot, coming in the same direction as if pursuing a fugitive, three hunters armed with rifles, booted and clad in the traditional leather garb with the long, curved feather in the hat. They are walking fast, in line abreast, along the water's edge, the blued-steel guns held in their left hands pointing downwards at an angle, ready to be raised, their right index fingers on the triggers. Having crossed the picture from left to right, but moving much more quickly, they too, with one stride, pass behind me.

Almost immediately a shot rings out in the silence, apparently very close, followed without any interval by a sharp cry like the rending call of a gull, though none is present; then there is a long-drawn-out whinny and a second, identical detonation, clear and violent, in which I recognize the combat Mauser used by the auxiliary militia, putting a brutal end to the plaintive wail that had been going on and on, a sound almost human, calling to mind that made in the forest by the fine animal with the flesh-coloured plumage known here as the bird-woman. There is nothing after that but jumbled sounds of water that has been set swirling by some falling body, or heavy footsteps, or by the sea beating furiously against an unexpected rock, mingling its eddies and the slaps of abruptly converging waves with the galloping of the crazed horse whose whinnies, briefer now, are already less distinct.

With calm restored, the surface flat again, the atmosphere once more one of waiting, in the almost imperceptible whistling of the wind, another pelican, flying along laboriously and silently just above the water, crosses the picture in a straight, receding line parallel to

10

the shore, the same distance out as the first, disturbingly duplicating its precise passage. Also following a parallel course and moving in the same direction, but this time a little farther out to sea, a third, similar bird then flies off with the same slowness; seeming to swim through the dense, translucent air, which it beats indolently with its weary wings, immutable, it eventually dissolves like the other two in the murky irresolution of the horizon away to the left. On the terrace of rough planks laid not edge to edge but with a gap between them varying from one finger to two, the greyish sand continues to progress in a steady, methodical, surreptitious manner in wavy, shifting tongues that advance noiselessly and relentlessly towards me.

Going in the same direction as the pelicans, the young beggar-prostitute now makes her entrance, as she does every day at the same time, with the gracefully lilting, dancer's step that enables me to identify her at first glance the instant she comes into my field of vision. I draw myself up cautiously with the aid of my stick, abandoning all discretion, in order to see her better: clad as usual in a long dress of white silk flowing in tatters, and following the line formed by the very edge of the waves, she is today dragging behind her over the sand with its litter of varied debris a limp thing, difficult to identify, that looks like an old fur coat, or like the skin of a wild animal, freshly flayed. The girl is already in almost full back view when she comes to a halt, the bare foot behind her resting only on its very tip and exposing its tiny, wave-washed sole in an upright position; then, very slowly, she rotates her statue-like bust and her face, pale as pink mother-of-pearl, towards me.

The lost look in her large eyes with their greeny-grey highlights appearing to gaze through me at some strange sight lying in my direction but beyond, I eventually follow her example and turn my face with its false beard (but still in my opinion unrecognizable) towards the board fence bounding that side of the esplanade of the phantom café, where all I can see is a defaced poster advertising the Michelet Circus, the name of which is still legible in large, lascivious capitals above fragments of the famous lithograph depicting a ravishing equestrienne in a white-gauze tutu and rose-pink tights tilting with a lance at an enraged bull.

At this point I hear behind me, probably carried by the wind, the clearly enunciated sentence, 'The great aurochs is dead,' the highly individual modulations of which put me in mind of the soft, musical voice of the mendicant enchantress. I turn my head back towards her, at least towards where she was a moment ago, for she has disappeared, leaving no further discernible trace in the bumpy surface of the sand than that made just now by the animal skin two paces in from the water's edge: a long, sinuous trail in which I believe I can make out dark patches of blood here and there.

As if without thinking, I sit down mechanically on a metal folding chair with chipped and rusting slats that is there right beside me, it too abandoned in this out-of-season landscape: an ancient city after the flood of burning ash, a village square the morning after the air-raid, a seaside resort half destroyed by equinoctial storms.

I cannot, however, contrive to fix my attention in a sufficiently convincing manner on the flakes of dull, pale-green paint that, where they have come away, have left constellations of red-brown triangles all over this disc of sheet metal that forms the top of a table on which my left elbow has just come to rest. I raise my eyes, which I had been holding too determinedly lowered. The two police-men are there, in plain clothes but clearly recognizable with their light-coloured raincoats belted with casual haste and their soft hats with broad brims turned down in front. I have the impression that this scene has occurred at least once before, so familiar do I find the picture it presents.

To tell the truth I had hardly had time to scan the deserted beach at length in an attempt to make out the already distant figure of the little prostitute in her shredded white veils, still fluttering at the edge of the waves. The two silhouettes were there, quietly menacing, right by my table, blocking the view with massive shoulders made even broader by their trench coats. They too appear to be used to the way the episode unfolds; it is almost with a smile of connivance that the first one holds out a pair of regulation handcuffs while his twin brother places before my eyes a rectangle of paper bearing a black-and-white photograph.

In spite of the document's curiously impressive size and the abnormal flimsiness of its support, my first thought is that this is a licence certifying that my visitors are indeed policemen. Closer examination, however, enables me to establish that this photo is not at all an identity portrait of the person standing before me: what I have here is quite simply a newspaper cutting in which a few words of text accompany a fairly mediocre snap taken by a reporter in what appears to be a factory, as witness the winches, cables, chains, and pulleys of all sizes distinguishable with some clarity towards the top of the frame. But the most remarkable thing in this setting, although situated neither in the centre of the composition nor in the foreground, is a very young woman, more than half undressed, hanging by the neck, which is slightly

13

twisted to one side, from a rope attached to an enormous iron tackle hook. I don't flinch.

On the side opposite that towards which the head with its long, tawny-gold hair is tilted the two half-extended arms, chained together at the wrist, hang at face height from a second, identical hook. Despite the shortage of light, very noticeable in the lower part of the print, I find on moving nearer that the victim still has the tips of her bare feet resting on two small round stools placed side by side about fifty centimetres apart and similar at all points to those used by women who operate drilling, grinding, buffing, and other similar machines, these frail (temporary?) supports preventing the captive from being actually strangled by the hemp rope. Shown from the front, she is wearing nothing but a pair of thin white-linen trousers torn several times from the waist down to the level of the crotch, large shreds of material having even been ripped away to reveal more of the stomach and the pubis with its triangle of fine, red-brown fleece; one thigh is exposed almost to the knee, and only the fact that the legs are spread stops what is left of the garment promptly slipping down round the ankles.

From the position of this exceedingly pretty machinist and the dangerously arousing curves of her proffered body, I see immediately that this is a trap: the native girl that the hunters tie to a stick embedded in the shallows of the backwater to attract the crocodile. I have all the more reason for showing prudence in that the graceful line of the throat and the soft curvature of the arms curiously reproduce the improbable pose of a famous painting, the pride of our National Museum: The Fair Angélique, chained to her rock, eyes wide with a blend of terror and surrender, gazing on the hunter whose lance at the last moment stops a monstrous reptile that was about to eat

14

her alive, at which point she emits a long-drawn-out, throaty moan as if the burning steel were sunk in her own vagina offered there as prey.

But in place of the giant alligator there is a violin lying on the ground, its melodious tones having perhaps been meant to blend with the cries of the victim. That at least will be one interpretation considered by the investigating authorities when they come across the instrument (riddled, let's not forget, with little holes quite unlike the tunnels made by wood-eating insects) abandoned a few paces from this soft-skinned nude now lying lifeless, in a position we shall have to come back to, amid the steel machines and their gear-wheels, the welding torches, and the blacksmith's tongs.

For the moment, however, all is silent, discounting the tiny, bell-like sound of the drops of water falling one after another into a pool, as already mentioned, though the precise nature of the liquid involved calls for closer examination, as has been said, or as will be said later, I don't remember. But this apparent calm does not catch me unawares. Here and there in the gloom shiny surfaces gleam with metallic highlights, shifting and changing as with increased circumspection I advance towards the bait.

While reluctant to admit as much, I am fascinated by her white-china complexion, her large, dark-ringed eyes, her sea-green irises staring at me without a quiver of an eyelid, playing to perfection the part of slavish submission and ecstatic entreaty, her lips parted as if to plead for mercy, or for forgiveness, yet not daring to say a word or make the slightest movement for fear of putting an end to the unstable equilibrium of the tall stools perched on their three slender legs, which forces her taut body to arch in what is in any case a most attractive fashion.

15

What will intrigue the police even more when they come to ascertain the facts and then seek an expert opinion is the virtual certainty that strangulation cannot have been the real cause of death, as indeed should have been seen at first glance from the dead girl's still pearl-white complexion and from the unobtrusive nature of the marks left on the skin of her long, pliant neck by the rope still encircling it. Nor is a single one of her fragile vertebrae broken. Moreover her whole silken, still warm body appears intact. One might just, if one looked carefully enough, note a great many tiny bright-pink dots, closer together in some areas than in others, that would appear to be needle-marks. As for the rest of the setting, it certainly has its surprising elements; the idea strikes me that I may have intruded upon some ceremony in the midst of its meticulous course. So am I the mysterious criminal at second hand who comes on the scene afterwards to finish off the torture?

Naturally I allowed no hint of these reflections to appear to the two plain-clothes policemen. I confined myself to asking them, as a trifle of no consequence, whether the traces of blood had been analysed or not. No one having so far made the slightest allusion to these faint reddish streaks staining the tips of the fingernails, the mouth, and the insides of the thighs without, apparently, any corresponding wound, it was difficult for me to say more: to point out to them, for example, that they might belong to a different blood group from that of the beautiful stranger, who in that case perhaps died as a result of drinking blood that was incompatible with her own, or of heart failure while battling tooth and claw against the monster, whose lingam she evidently succeeded in damaging, or anything else of that sort.

In reality I am much more interested in the matter of

the fur coat. Had it gone when the police arrived? Above all, how was it still there when I came along myself? Such an oversight would be most unlikely on the part of an organization that has only too often shown proof of scrupulous care in the allotment of tasks with a view to their precise and prompt execution. Unfortunately I did not have time, before leaving in rather more of a hurry than usual, to examine in detail what looked like a ceremonial cloak made from a big-cat skin, or the skin of some other animal having thick, curly hair all down the front of its body; the object, though conspicuous enough, was rolled up in a ball in one corner and had caught my eye only as, much to my regret, I was having as a matter of urgency to search for a secret exit by which to make my escape.

The more I think about it, the surer I am that this was the same garment as is now being dragged along the beach in front of me by the enigmatic beggar prostitute, with whom I decided without hesitation to fall into step in order to examine at rather less of a distance this blood-stained skin with which she is sweeping the sand: its very full shape remains as distinctive as its warm, red-gold colour, which is the more striking, despite the powdered shell adhering among the fur and gluing it together in flaxen hanks, for reproducing the exact copper-blond tint of the girl's unkempt hair. Seeing her from behind like this, I also notice that she has under her arms, pressed against her hip, an old violin without its case. I understand immediately why she has that curious set of the neck noted earlier: it betrays her professional habit of holding the instrument pinched between collar-bone and chin.

Her pace having been too brisk for me to be able to follow her for long over ground so soft that my stick sank into it, I return slowly to the terrace of the abandoned café. Two men in light-coloured trench coats and felt hats have sat down at a table as if awaiting the return of a hypothetical waiter wearing a white jacket and carrying napkin and tray. There is something so comical about their situation in this wilderness that it seems to me preferable to ignore their presence. As soon as I reach the board floor, which is firmer despite the little dunes encroaching on it, I bear right, that is to say in the direction of the old spa hotel.

I was wrong about the torn poster, the remains of which are mixed up with the property advertisements and "Wanted" notices on the boundary fence: it is not a bull that the equestrienne is fighting but a gigantic iron-grey cayman, which has opened towards her its disproportionately large red mouth, so bright it appears to be spitting fire, while the colt, ridden without stirrups or saddle, rears up in alarm, splashing up on all sides the shallow water of a circular pool that entirely fills the stage for this still very popular act.

All down the rows of seats from top to bottom the spectators sit tense and silent, in contrast to what happens in the arenas of the Ancient World. And one can hear the tiniest sounds of the contest without difficulty. The fiery virgin has just lost her balance, hampered by the too-long lance as her intractable mount was turning abruptly, and the enormous reptile, endowed by the sheet of water with quite incredible agility, stands up for an instant on its tail and its short legs to snatch this delicious prey and swallow it at one gulp.

It is at this moment when I am least expecting it, utterly absorbed as I am by so stimulating and dangerous a spectacle, that I feel the two large hands laid firmly on my arms, one from each side, gradually squeezing me in a

18

double vice just above the elbows. I don't need to look at these neighbours flanking me with their impressively broad shoulders to know without risk of being mistaken who they are and what they want of me. A drawing, even one on Ingres paper, would be entirely superfluous.

The only thought that might still be of some importance concerns the little device producing the magnetic signal that opens the black door of the sanctuary: having unfortunately been left in the inside pocket of the white jacket I am wearing today, it is going to fall into their hands.

I remain absolutely motionless, as prescribed. Nor do the other two attempt the least movement. It's another impasse.

So the story will have to be re-started earlier than originally intended.

Motionless, I said. That is indeed one's prevailing feeling now on entering this quarter that consists of no more than five or six little streets miraculously preserved amid the ruins and the waste ground—a few kitchen gardens have even been laid out here and there between the heaps of rubble—preserved, then, and carefully maintained on account of the historical interest of buildings that all go back to the early years of the nineteenth century and are thus very old for this part of the world.

The central avenue (if so pompous a name can suitably be bestowed on a thoroughfare of such modest length and devoid of all traffic) slopes sufficiently to make little flights of two or three granite steps necessary to restore a horizontal surface in front of each doorstep. It is spring already, the southern spring, and a still pale sun shines softly green on the new foliage of the chestnut trees. The air is mild, all sounds far-off and quiet. It is Sunday. At regular intervals a solitary, invisible bird (a phoenix thrush?) re-starts his song, only to break it off again in the middle, each time at a different point of the same long phrase that dies away in a few faltering notes as if the bird had forgotten the rest. No one is ever seen in this street, although the two or three storeys of all the houses are—it seems—occupied, one is tempted to say for residential purposes.

The story as written up in an article in *The Globe* starts off like a fairy-tale. A chief inspector by the name of Franck V. Francis, off-duty that day and striding along with no precise route or destination in mind, finds in the street in question, which he happens to be passing down for the first time in his life in the course of this adventurous morning walk, a lady's shoe in a very small size lying abandoned on one of those cast-iron gratings with arabesque perforations, designed for watering the trees, that have survived in certain districts dating from the colonial period . . . There, we seem to be off to a good start this time.

Brisk and unsuspecting, he picks up the object, which hardly looks like one of the bits of refuse that frequently spill from the bins during the over-hasty collections made in the early mornings by the municipal dustcarts; on the contrary it is practically new, all except for the heel, which is damaged near the bottom and has almost parted from the sole, an accident easily repaired—even by an amateur—with the aid of a hammer and three nails, a job that would be all the more justified in view of the fact that this is clearly an expensive article imported from Europe: a delicate evening or dress shoe in a beautiful ocean blue with just a hint of green, hand-made from the supple stomach hide of a farm-reared cayman and decorated, in the middle of the upper, with a large, imitation-stone cabochon, triangular in shape and an amazing golden colour with metallic highlights.

Closer examination further reveals a small reddish stain on the right side of the pointed tip, clearly outlined and forming a slight bulge on the turquoise skin like a drop of dried blood, though one that could scarcely have come from a wound on the foot itself, given its position. As for the very fresh marks of some slight scratching round the bottom of the heel, they make it possible to reconstruct the trivial incident in which the lady lost her shoe: the shoe (her left one) had caught in a hole in the cast-iron grating and the fragile heel had been partially torn off by being pulled out too sharply. But why had this clumsy person not subsequently recovered her property? When she could have patched things up for the time being and gone on her way, putting that foot down with slightly greater care from then on, why had she chosen to saunter on, hobbling on one shoe? Was that the whimsical behaviour of opera-goers returning home from the theatre very late at night, or possibly from the Michelet Circus, which at that time used to organize evening entertainments on a grand scale? Possibly this is yet another case of one of those wealthy foreigners who go about slightly drunk or under the influence of some allegedly mood-elevating drug and whose eccentricities the newspapers report daily.

Franck V. Francis has reached this point in his reflections when he notices other identical little brown splashes, dry yet shiny, presenting a polished surface and therefore very recent because no dust has had time to dull them, dotting the pavement as far as a flight of granite steps, slightly more numerous on the steps themselves where the wounded woman would have waited for a few moments while the door was being opened to her. Wanting to ring himself, the inspector then discovers that this door has no call system and, even more curiously, neither handle nor lock. Situated on the odd side between nos. 9 and 11, the house has no number either but instead a stone eye carved the wrong way up.

Our policeman hazards a knock on the wood, freshly painted black, and is disconcerted by the brazen sound given off by the panel, which is evidently not made of oak and most certainly not of pine. But despite the deep, voluminous echo that seems to reverberate beneath huge vaults loudly enough to rouse the whole building, no one opens the door to him. Nor does anyone appear at the windows (two on the ground floor down the street from the entrance and three on each of the first and second floors), which suddenly begin to look like decorative imitations: beyond the panes of ancient glass whose bumps and highlights make it hard to see through them, Inspector Francis thinks he can in places see the brick wall continuing behind the sham casement, which has been built out over it.

Deciding to come back the next day, a weekday, with an armed colleague and a formal search warrant, he continues his stroll in the direction of the sea, which he is surprised to find so close, at the end of an alley with no houses but lined with hoardings. This brings him out on the front by the old hydropathic, a de luxe hotel that has been out of use for a long time and that had its interior appointments ransacked and three-parts destroyed by the bands of runaway children who moved in with their weapons and horses after the war against Uruguay; in fact it became necessary after a few months to exterminate them systematically on account of the spectacular crimes and misdemeanours that the more audacious among them, if not the older ones, were beginning to perpetrate well beyond the zone tacitly abandoned to fringe elements, drug addicts, and perverts not amenable to any control as well as to the developers of the future. Soaring above the deserted beach is a large imperial vulture of the variety known as "firebird" on account of a legend that credits them with being able to fly into the sooty flames of carrion incinerators in order to seize their food from the fire ready-roasted. Here, however, the flesh-eating raptor's presence is easily explained by the large dead fish that the sea has been washing up for several days round all this part of the bay.

The very next morning Franck V. Francis sets out to return to his suspicious house, the black door of which has plagued him incessantly all night long. He takes the precaution of getting an expert in electronic locks and safes to accompany him. But although he spends hours wandering through vast areas under demolition he is no longer able to find the marvellous island of calm, nor the short, sloping avenue shaded by mature planes, nor the Directoire-style buildings preserved by the town-planning authorities. Moreover his assistant assures him that he has never heard of an old quarter anywhere in this sector. Franck would certainly think he had been dreaming were the delicate blue shoe with the golden stone not there in the bottom of his raincoat pocket, carefully wrapped in a semi-transparent plastic bag, to vouch for the reality of what he remembers with the precision of an engraving.

He goes back to Opera House Square with the intention of tracing exactly the route taken from the old bridge the day before. The muddy waters of the river, swollen by the spring rains, were battling yesterday as they are today against the rising tide. But this morning, leaning against the stone parapet, there was a very young girl—twelve or thirteen years old, possibly, and quite pretty despite the slovenliness of her dress, or on the contrary because of it—selling roses singly. Her left arm steadied a light tray that was made out of a fruiterer's crate suspended from her neck on a length of perished hemp rope, while with her right hand she presented, slightly to one side at breast height, a single bloom held vertically in the way one sees in Renaissance paintings in museums, which is where the child's faraway look also seemed to have come from, the child herself being frozen in her hieratic pose as if crushed under the whole ancestral weight of it.

This image disturbed the inspector without his knowing quite why. He had the impression that he recognized her as a figure familiar to him from his everyday life, and yet he could have sworn she had not been there or anywhere else the day before or on any other day. Unless his memory wholly deceived him he believed he could state that he had never seen the little girl before. He was reminded of the slogan of the security forces, "Never trust a child!" but he did not manage to laugh at it with much enthusiasm.

In desperation he returned to his office, where he dared not say too much about his discovery and his disappointment for fear of being made fun of. No disappearance of a young lady from the fashionable world had been entered in the registers. To take his mind off the problem he began studying the file on the suspect cans of salmon in piquant sauce under investigation for containing the flesh of animals poisoned by nocturnal effluent from the very factories where they were canned, ramshackle installations

24

situated at the edge of the water into which they poured illicit by-products every evening after the last shift had gone home.

And it was not until three days later that they had found, floating half-submerged at the foot of the cliff that closes off the northern end of the longest of the beaches, the body of a girl whose ample head of hair, blond with russet highlights, mingled with the veils and threads of seaweed bobbing on the swell in one of those holes about ten metres deep that communicate with the open sea beneath the piled-up rocks. Franck had then remembered the imperial vulture spotted in the vicinity the previous Sunday. He had thought about it even more insistently when the exceptionally small size of the drowned girl's feet was pointed out to him.

Arriving on the scene when the forensic pathologist— that day it was Dr. Morgan—had already taken his instruments from his black-leather bag and spread them out in the centre of the large flat rock overlooking the irregular hollow in the granite, where it formed a sort of natural swimming-pool, Franck had not been able to stand seeing the surgeon carry out the routine preliminary investigations on the smooth white body laid out in full daylight, polished like a piece of marble, a classical statue with eyes wide open and not a trace of swelling or bruising to disfigure it. Reluctant to admit a discomfiture that was incomprehensible in view of the job he did and the kind of sight that was all in a day's work to him, he had recovered his composure and at the same time found an alibi in gazing at the blue water, which was full of eddies and gilded undulations and too deep for him to see the bottom.

He had then returned by way of the Grand Spa Hotel, once famous for its thousand and one luxurious rooms

25

ranged on either side of interminable corridors, the massive but now partially burnt-out silhouette of which was with time and progressive dilapidation taking on an increasingly ghostly appearance.

Next day he had learned that, soon after his departure from the cliff, one of the large black dogs belonging to the police, which for an hour had been sniffing among the pools and in the crevices between the rounded rocks and the clumps of seaweed smelling of iodine in search of unlikely trails, had fetched in its mouth from somewhere or other a delicate, blue, crocodile-skin shoe in a very small size. The trimming—knot, rosebud, or cabochon— had been torn off. Contrary to Franck's expectations (in fact he had only checked the detail for form's sake, so sure had he been of the answer), this was again a left shoe, the heel of which had become half detached in some mad chase, or fall, or fight . . . or what else? Unable to bear it any longer and at the risk of giving away, when there is no real need to do so, an identity hitherto kept cleverly concealed, I run home and pull open the draw with the false bottom. Everything is in place in the secret compartment: the little register covered with black oil-cloth, the needles and syringes, the keys to the Cadillac and the other two cars, etc. But the transparent plastic bag, in which I kept her evening shoe to remind me of the woman called Angelica, is empty.

I telephone the office. Morgan answers. No, the girl didn't drown; she was already dead on entering the water, where she spent not several days but barely two or three hours. You could always, the doctor adds, claim it was a case of an overdose, because she had quite a few pretty odd things in her blood. (Does the fool suspect something?) No further details? asks Inspector Francis with as much detachment as he can still muster. No, apart from a

26

punctured pink-rubber beach ball that the second dog had found and that, according to him, had also belonged to the victim.

Franck V. Francis feels a sudden hollowness inside, a rush of blood to his head, and his legs giving way: the abrupt surfacing to consciousness of an irreparable false move made in the last few days, or at least in his account of them. He stammers several unintelligible words and replaces the receiver. He sits down on the first support within reach (the heavy brass-bound trunk!), but without managing to recover his normal faculties.

He is overcome by a falling sensation: a drop of the kind experienced in nightmares, when the ground one expects to reach at any moment instead subsides further and further beneath feet deprived of their function. From what abyss will he have afterwards to re-begin? This is the last sentence that flashes through his mind, with the soldiers of the special militia already hammering at the armour-plated door, just before he loses consciousness.

Right at the outset there is a kind of commotion, a confusion of bodies in jumbled movement, men in dark uniforms jostling one another as they advance, or more probably jostling someone else, dragging that person with them down an indistinct, pale-coloured, quite wide corridor or even a number of corridors with no features by which they might be differentiated, though of progressively narrower dimensions and succeeding one another at right angles with sudden changes of direction

27

for no apparent reason, irregularly and in a manner impossible to predict.

The trampling, the flailing of arms or legs mingled in a shapeless mass moving forward rapidly if chaotically, the rustle of the black uniforms, the heavy breathing, all disappear from one second to the next—and all that is left afterwards is, again, the empty, almost abstract corridor, it too, one would think, about to fade away, painted an undistinguished, lustreless white—but it all reappears immediately in another, perpendicular corridor, narrower still in all probability, almost making it difficult for the milling group to pass. How many of them are there? The struggling and the over-animated gesturing make it impossible to say even approximately: five or six, perhaps, fifteen or so, or more, or far fewer.

The passage is so small at this point that the heavy boots are marking time; the throng of black tunics is compacted into what amounts to an elongated plug scratching the blind walls with its many gilt buttons, tabbed epaulettes, and stiff leather belts, each of which supports symmetrically a bulging cartridge pouch and a fat holster with its regulation pistol. Once past the corner, however, everything having dispersed as if by magic, the momentarily agitated space is once more white and empty. Afterwards, a little farther on, there is a fresh commotion of military uniforms rushing along in disarray, then the empty corridor once more, and again the violent, confused troop, the empty corridor, the troop surging forward, the empty corridor, etc.

And at last it all comes up against something, a door opening under the pressure of the first members of the group to reach it. The black boots laced up to the calf have gradually, over the space of several seconds, come to a halt; the jodhpurs in turn are still. A residue of movement continues to affect the mass above the patent-leather belts, the chests buttoned up in the straight tunics with little stand-up collars, the arms with their oblique braid stripe, the hands in black-leather gloves that appear to be driving out some foreign body located in the middle of the party, disturbing the surface—at the level of the stiff-looking flat caps—with an eddy whose centre moves forward in irregular meanderings, eventually expelling the intruder all of a sudden, like a pip being spat out or a cork being blown by too much pressure in the bottle. This too is a man, though very different from the others (he is wearing white pyjamas), and the door shuts behind him with a dull thud. Once again the dangerous stir has ceased completely; but for how long?

Yet nothing more occurs. The soldiers, however many there were of them, their faces empty, their loose-fitting garments lacking any distinguishing shape or markings, have vanished for good. Who said they were soldiers, even?

The man is alone in the silence, standing in the middle of the cell. And bit by bit, almost cautiously, I ascertain that it is probably myself. That apart, there is nothing to report except the two small windows, too high up and fitted with strong grilles, a wooden chair painted white, a broken mirror, nothing else. On reflection, the presence of the looking-glass is unusual in this type of locality. I go over to the wall and lean forward towards its clouded, greenish surface, which is roughly trapezoidal in shape: bounded on the top by two right angles with ground edges and by a slightly curved oblique line with a sharp edge forming the bottom. I have some trouble recognizing myself in the image framed there. My hair must have been shaved off, but several days ago already, and a uniform dark shadow covers my skull, cheeks, and chin.

I run the tips of three outstretched fingers slowly over the chief features of the proffered face: the chin, the right half of the mouth (the lower lip from the middle to the corner, then the upper lip back to the middle), the inner rim of the right nostril, the wing and bridge of the nose, the superciliary arch. They are my features, without doubt. But the face as a whole seems to me to have lost all character and identity; it's a standard face, an anonymous shape; it makes me look like that identikit portrait of the murderer that was in the papers and that made me laugh so much not so very long ago as, clean-shaven and with my hair freshly groomed, dressed in grey with that discreet and confidence-inspiring elegance I have always had occasion to congratulate myself on, having left my car in a space where parking is "permitted for a few moments during off-peak periods" and crossed the promenade with the stiff, springy gait of the seriously disabled, which I now execute to perfection leaning on a special ivory-handled stick, and having subsequently, and with much deliberation, picked out a table on its own but exposed to the morning sun on the almost deserted terrace of one of the many establishments lining the sea-front, been met by a black waiter dressed in immaculate white who took upon himself to offer in the most accommodating manner the seat selected by this wealthy, crippled customer, and ordered from him a large white coffee and two brioches, I settled myself more comfortably in my cane armchair with my left leg stretched out in front of me and a little to one side, preparatory to perusing in detail, with the scrupulous care I invest in this sort of thing as in many others, the article in the latest, nine-o'clock edition of *The Globe*.

I spot the first anomaly immediately: the face, which is drawn in a black line on a grey background, is distinctly asymmetrical, yet this not insignificant fact is mentioned neither in the consequent general description nor in any of the various statements taken from witnesses. Going on to read the text, I see that the position of the body is not right either, nor its location in the vast workshop of the derelict factory. It is difficult to draw any definite conclusions at this stage since, to explain these changes, at least three solutions appear possible (although, to tell the truth, none of them is entirely convincing): mis-reporting by the journalist concerned, moving of the body by someone else subsequently to the crime, deliberate lying by the police with a view to misleading or hoodwinking or un-nerving the criminal or criminals.

Nevertheless I experience a mild feeling of excitement at reading about one detail of the setting attributed wrongly to the killer and furnishing evidence of an interesting fancy on the part of the person who turned up afterwards, or the writer of the article, or a crafty policeman. But there I sense the trap straight away . . . Wanting once more to take stock of the question of a possible return to the scene, I raise my eyes towards the bright line of the horizon marking the upper limit of a flat, blue sea that is also bordered, down below, by the shimmering fringe produced by tiny wavelets; the beach has an absent air at this time of day, whereas around noon it is suddenly teeming with people, a protected hunting-ground where I have only to lie down in the sand—this time with no disability and no stick—to take my pick entirely at my leisure from the endless procession of bronzed and more than half-naked beach girls: that one, for example, a fine specimen, unusually fair for these parts, today playing ball with two other girls without appearing to be bothered by the crowd's unpredictable interventions in the game, which on the contrary provoke

31

endless cries of delight, I've been watching her for several weeks now, on and off, noting her lithe contortions, the gorgeous swirl of her hair, her deep-throated laugh.

At this point, however, while returning my gaze to the folded page held stiffly in front of me with both hands, I find that a customer on her own—a student, it seems—has without my noticing the fact sat down at a table not far from my own, evidently while I was absorbed in my meticulous examination of the newspaper. She has placed a book and a notebook, both closed and covered with black paper, on the white tablecloth that four metal clips secure in place against sudden gusts of wind. Here I narrowly avoid branching off in the direction of the short-lived miniature tornado that convulses the crowded beach and go on to observe that, also in front of the young student, placed to one side near the edge of the circular table, there are a glass and a bottle (opened but still full) of the red soft drink containing stimulants that universities consume in large quantities at examination time. How can this last-minute arrival have been served already when I have been aware of no comings and goings by staff on the terrace and have not yet seen the black waiter return with my own order?

At this moment, as if sensing that she is being watched, although my position is some way behind her own, the girl slowly turns her head in my direction; the perfection, the assurance of her movement immediately convince me that she knew in advance the whereabouts of the object on which her eyes would come to rest; she stares at me for an instant, then, without a flicker of expression, she calmly rotates her shoulders and neck back to gaze once more at the almost artificial stillness of the sunlit sea, straight ahead of her. Full, well-defined lips, large pale eyes, a very long neck, small ears, smooth, warm skin, the

32

curves of her body firm and without heaviness, altogether she corresponds pretty closely to the type of entry headed "ripe-fleshed adolescent". The better, it would seem, to show off a bosom whose roundness—seen in profile—appears to owe nothing to a bra, she proceeds to execute an elaborate and unpredictable gesture with her two bare arms, which rise slowly in the shape of an amphora above her thick black hair with its russet highlights, touching wrists for a moment and afterwards separating them again in a double revolution of the hands such as oriental dancing-girls perform, the elbows then starting to fall forward and down, lower and lower, until they land softly on the tablecloth, where the forearms remain extended on either side of the black notebook. In its affected complexity this graceful movement, which moreover—since there is no one else around—may have been aimed at the stranger with the greying temples, whose delicate hands and steel-rimmed spectacles suggest the surgeon, with a view to exciting his interest (message received, aha!), though purely in fun rather than in a spirit of calculation, this movement strikes me as a sign that will probably decide the girl's fate. I now have to see her standing and also study the way she walks. It's my move, then. Meanwhile the girl again turns in my direction; and for the second time I feel myself become the one subjected to petrifying observation.

There is a square judas measuring about twenty centimetres each way in the door of my cell. The warders outside can either open the whole thing in order to pass a bowl or some other object in to the prisoner or they can simply operate—to greater or lesser effect—the shutter system with which the hinged leaf is fitted: five heavy iron slats pivoting on themselves about their horizontal axes. Between the second and third of these slats, which at present are slanting at forty-five degrees (without my having seen them move or heard the least sound of footsteps in the corridor), framed in the darkness beneath the little metal visor, are the two bright, expressionless, staring eyes of someone looking in.

Surveillance must be part of the overall plan here for changing the prisoners, together with the injections, the incomprehensible questioning, and the jostling along the corridors. Now, though, we have the iron slats closing soundlessly with a slow, smooth movement until eventually they overlap one another by eight or ten millimetres. When there is no longer the least interstice (the sharpest knife would not find the tiny crack to prise it open), the whole flap swings open to admit a man's arm holding a sort of small register covered with black paper. Instead of being dressed in the sleeve of a uniform with gilt buttons, the arm is bare, quite pale but very muscular, and covered with hair. After a second's hesitation over how to behave in these unforeseen circumstances, I take two steps towards the closed door and seize the black book. The arm is immediately withdrawn and the judas shuts again, this time with a sharp bang. After that we have the shutter slats slowly opening once more.

I recognize the book: outwardly at least it is the one that the false student placed near her in the centre of the small, circular table on the café terrace and on the cover of which five slim fingers with pink fingernails play nonchalantly as, still looking behind her in my direction, she continues her critical, searching, interested, at any rate probably attentive examination of me. Although I sustain her gaze without difficulty (which is not to say without impatience), the girl is slow to turn away, being to all appearances unimpressed by my diagnosis as a practitioner contemplating her already quartered on the polished-steel operating-table, where thin straps of black leather hold her motionless.

Decision taken. Keeping my eyes on her, I point with my right hand, still in its black-leather glove, towards my outstretched stiff leg and my polished-steel walking-stick. I say, "Excuse me. I have difficulty in getting about, and I have left my cigarettes in the car." I then indicate the gleaming Cadillac parked along the promenade. The student, without a feature of her glossy sex-magazine face moving, without a hint of a smile twisting her mouth with its pinky-brown rims or the long, curved lashes batting even once over the light green of her large eyes, the false student directs her translucent gaze successively at my orthopaedic stick, at the big black car, and finally back at myself; likewise avoiding the smallest unnecessary gesture, I carry my hand to the right pocket of my jacket and, with the slowness of the butterfly hunter who is fearful of alarming a rare Vanessa, a gorgeous, downy creature, by over-hasty handling of his net, extract from it a bunch of keys that I hold out to the stranger suspended between thumb and forefinger by the smallest one of all, the one that opens the off-side front door. "Would you be so kind as to fetch them for me?"

She looks at me, weighs my overbearingly paternal smile, considers what may lie behind such a mask (that of a harmless doctor of gynaecology, or a psycho-somatician), appraises the disturbing and confidence-inspiring car, assesses whether it is humanly possible to refuse an invalid this small service . . . I add, "From the glove compartment."

Still failing to show any sign whatever of communication or intelligence, the girl gets up and comes towards me, takes my keys without a word, turns and winds her way between the tables and chairs to the wide pavement, walks straight over to the car, bends down to insert the key, etc.

Excellent postures, lithe, pleasing walk, perfect figure; a special mention for a pair of very long legs with bare thigh visible between the high white boots and a thin dress of bronzed silk, the lower part of which is reduced to the minimum in the fashion of that year. Having performed the various movements precisely and without embellishment, though aware, as she was bending over with one knee on the front seat to reach the glove compartment, of revealing a pair of apricot-coloured briefs enhanced by a scarcely indicated twist of the hips, she soon comes back holding out to me the shiny keys and the little blue packet, obviously already open.

"Thank you," I say. And as if automatically, with great naturalness, I pull out several cigarettes, at the same time offering her the chance to take one. She hesitates. Her fate is in the balance. She takes a cigarette between two fingers. With a quick glance I check that it is not the one with a tiny red mark on the end of the filter, which I promptly select for myself, of course. And with the gold lighter that I have taken with my other hand from the left pocket of my jacket, where at the same time I stowed the packet, I light the two cigarettes one after the other. The girl bows and goes back to her seat. So shall I never know what her voice sounds like?

It's only then that I become aware of the mistake of which I have just taken the first step: as a general rule I ought never to limp in this type of scene. But it's too late. The effect is very swift, because the student inhales the smoke and holds it in her lungs for a long time before slowly expelling it. At the third puff she passes a hand across her forehead as if her head were spinning, which must be more or less what is happening. Not wasting a minute (knowing the very brief duration of the drug's action), I get up and with the aid of my stick—which it is now impossible for me to forget—go over to where my victim has slumped back in her chair, a vague, corpse-like smile hovering over lips that have parted at last, her arms hanging down at either side, at random. The cigarette has fallen to the ground. A few furtive glances round about satisfy me that no one is taking any notice of us; I crush the glowing tip with the toe of my shoe and stoop— perhaps showing rather too much suppleness—to pick up this piece of incriminating evidence and slip it into a pocket, out of sight. Straightening up again, I see the waiter returning with my white coffee, his eyes on me, already quite close. Instead of completing my movement I grasp one of the student's hands in passing and pretend to be feeling the pulse, this time leaning ostentatiously on my stick. "This girl is feeling ill," I say.

The waiter starts complaining in a low voice, speaking in a language that must be South-American Portuguese. The girl, her dreams disturbed by this commotion around her, manages to utter the word "smoke". Before taking any action I wait to find out whether or not the other man has understood the meaning of this syllable, which may have been barely audible, especially to a foreigner.

"She said 'smoke'," the Negro gets out with difficulty after about ten seconds, in very uncertain English, staring at me in a vaguely fearful or suspicious manner. My response is immediate and brisk: "Yes, I thought as much. They all take it at the University now. But this one hasn't yet got the typical look of the regular user. Best to get her out of here as quickly as possible." Particularly since here come two inquisitive spectators already.

"We need a doctor," the waiter says.

"Has something happened?" the older of the new-comers asks. I must act firmly, leaving them no time to

37

take any kind of personal initiative, otherwise all will be lost. "I'm a doctor," I say, "and I have my car here. I'll take this young addict to the hospital as I have to go there anyway. Here, you'll have to carry her, the two of you, over to the Caddy there. It won't be the first time it's served as an ambulance!" If I may allow myself the metaphor! Aha! I add (and curiously it is this last argument that seems to persuade them to do as I say), "I'm unable to help you because of my leg."

Standing there beside the table on which the waiter has just deposited my brioches and my coffee with cream (and which is not in fact the one I had chosen), I relish the spectacle of these three kind souls carrying my prey all warm to its black-painted coffin. It is the Brazilian in the white jacket who has the girl under the armpits; the two bystanders, evidently not so strong, have taken a thigh each; since they are holding them higher than the rest of the body the golden dress, which is too short, has slid over the stomach, revealing a band of satiny skin of a delightful pale-brown colour (her whole body appears to be uniformly tanned) above the tiny briefs that just cover the pubis. Leaning on the steel stick, which I am holding firmly in my left hand, I unthinkingly break off a piece of the white bread and start dunking it in my cup.

I must have taken several sips, judging by the level of the liquid, and eaten a whole brioche, since there is now only one left on the white tablecloth, when I notice that the little group constituted as aforesaid is standing—but how long have they been there?—by the car, of which I forgot to give them the keys, with three pairs of eyes fixed on me. I hurriedly lay a few coins on the table beside the second, still intact brioche and go over to them, limping impeccably.

I get behind the wheel. The others lay the girl on the

seat beside me, I having first lowered the back by means of the automatic control button that instantly turns it into a bed. This unusual arrangement, coupled with the red caduceus adorning the windscreen, sets the seal on my assumed profession. Moreover the impressive size and serious-looking colour of the car give it an almost official air. Before starting off I take the time, beneath the solidified gazes of my porters, who have lapsed into immobility two paces from the body of the car, lined up as if on parade, to enter in the log under today's date the following few indispensable notes, which they cannot read from where they are standing: "0930 hours, Café Maximilian on the front, black Cadillac 432 AB 123, stiff left leg, ivory-handled stick, medium-grey suit, steel-rimmed spectacles, thin, grizzled moustache." To check this detail I run the tips of two outstretched fingers along my left upper lip from the middle to the corner of my mouth.

Suddenly I have the feeling of a throng of curious onlookers pressing against the tinted windows of the car, having probably run up from the beach, noiselessly on their bare feet, to join the three original witnesses, who are still standing motionless in the front row of the crowd. With a single movement I close the black book, which makes a slap like a shot. In front of me the slats of the judas are once again shut. But outside there is a trampling and a jostling. The narrow corridor must suddenly have become choked at one of its unpredictable changes of direction, where the mob of dark uniforms and heavy boots is instantly compressed into a tumultuous mass, the confusion of which further slows down its flow. Straining one's ears, one can make out a rustling of leather, thuds against the walls, metallic clicks, individual exclamations emerging here and there from a rumbling and as it were pent-up murmur that is like the sound of the sea; it gradually swells in intensity in a succession of waves, after several seconds becoming a roar, deafening but then abruptly cut off, once more giving way to silence. Ears pricked, I wait for the following change to take place, equally suddenly, unannounced . . . But nothing more occurs. Very carefully I open the black book near the middle.

A woman's handwriting, painstaking and clearly legible, covers the entire page, the little characters ranged in fine, regularly-spaced lines and bearing a title in the upper margin: Secret Properties of the Triangle. If the three sides of any triangle are extended to infinity in the six directions possible, the result is a plane. In that infinite plane the three apices of the triangle lie on a circle that wholly contains the triangle. The three sides of the triangle form tangents of a second common circle that is wholly contained within the triangle. The internal bisectors of the three angles intersect at the centre of this second circle, while the mid-perpendiculars of the three sides—which also admit of a common point—meet at the centre of the first. When these two points merge (concentric circles), the triangle is said to be equilateral.

A figure drawn carefully with compasses and ruler represents this particular case. Contrary to the usual practice of elementary geometry courses, the triangle is here placed point downwards. Having once more checked the solitude, the absolute tranquility of this part of town already described—this muddy clutter of derelict sites and ruins, punctuated by open spaces, where I have just stopped the big black car alongside a hoarding covered with multi-coloured posters hanging in shreds—but remaining in my seat in order to be able, in an emergency, to drive off immediately before the intruder has had time to notice my prisoner laid out beside me, working carefully and precisely with one hand only (my left hand is still resting on the steering-wheel) while leaning sideways towards the languid, prostrate body, I slit the golden dress axially with a single stroke of the scalpel from the triangle of orange silk (drawn out sideways towards the hips), the top edge of which just discloses the beginning of a fleece of fair hair (also triangular although smaller in size and much closer to the equilateral model), right up to the throat, where a little cross comes into view, held around the neck by its slender chain.

I proceed to part the two edges of the fringed rent that my blade has just opened up, I fold back the two flaps of material on either side, and I am able at first glance to verify three of my former hypotheses: the absence of any underwear or lingerie apart from the briefs already mentioned, the firmness of the young breasts, which even in the lying position fall only imperceptibly short of being perfectly hemispherical, and finally the uniform tan of skin that is remarkably fine, delicate, and soft to the touch. As I have already pointed out, if my recollections are correct, the girl was placed head forwards with the back of her neck resting on the very edge of the seat, so that her loose brown hair hangs in thick tresses to the floor.

I am suddenly struck by the anomaly represented by this hair colour, false brunettes being much scarcer than false blondes, particularly in this country. Two additional snicks with the scalpel, one on each side towards the top of the groin, confirm my suspicions by laying bare the perfect triangle of a silky bush as pale as straw, which was hidden beneath the superposed triangular mask of coarse silk or possibly satin, the colour of ripe apricots. The exposed body, having lost its last protective covering, is now

41

wearing only the high boots of soft white kid and the little gold cross. Turning my attention to the face, which is half thrown back, I believe I momentarily catch a slight movement of the green eyes, as if the lovely sleeper were surreptitiously observing me beneath the long lashes of her half-closed lids.

It's time, anyway, to add the longer-lasting effect of a proper injection to the temporary one of the cigarette. So without dwelling any further on considerations of discrepant pilosity I seize the syringe already prepared for injection from its self-opening case. The patient's position inhibiting convenient access to the traditional areas, I choose to make the injection in the tough, amber-coloured skin near the areola of the right breast; and in order to find out for certain, by causing her a very sharp pain in this particularly sensitive region, whether the girl is conscious or not, I push the needle in with deliberate slowness, rotating it like a gimlet. It seems to me that I detect a faint trembling of the belly, a quiver followed by tiny spasmodic contractions running along beneath the epidermis from the pit of the stomach to the pubis, a shudder that is continued (even becoming slightly more pronounced) when the too-thick liquid spurts deep into the flesh under pressure that is on the contrary much more brutal and rapid than was called for.

I watch my victim's sweet face with close attention. Surely the mouth is open wider now . . . And again I see the two dilated pupils staring at me. The second mistake I have made then hits me, for no reason, in all its obviousness: I left the student's book and notebook on the table next to the one at which I lingered to eat a brioche. It is undoubtedly going to be pretty easy in these circumstances to identify the missing girl and start looking for her. Also at this point there drifts through my mind a vague memory of the café waiter in his white jacket, seen through the window of the closed car door exchanging signs of complicity with his two ostensibly chance assistants as if in reality he knew them very well. As for my alleged prey, she may have kept the smoke in her mouth for a long time without inhaling it, precisely in order to mislead me, and just now she stoically put up with that cruel injection, in anticipation of which she had previously swallowed a powerful antidote . . .

At this precise moment I spot in the left wing mirror another black car parked at some distance behind my own in a clearly visible place where there was certainly nothing a moment ago. There being no more time for me to proceed to further tests of sensitivity on even more tender areas of my patient's body—though the results would be extremely useful to me for subsequent operations—I rev up the engine, which has been idling all this time, only to become aware immediately of something different about the cylinder noise, which as a rule is very much smoother. I drive off none the less, not even taking the time to pull out the little syringe, which is still stuck upright in my awkward passenger's breast, so deeply did I sink the needle in it.

There is no question now, in the circumstances, of making the projected delivery to the fake shop, which I pass without slowing down and without so much as glancing at the dummies in their filmy, translucent white dresses who smile engaging in the windows. Leaving the ruined quarter behind me, I re-cross—this time in the other direction—the bridge over the swollen river. The little flower-seller, trying to move me, holds out at arm's length the single rosebud she has left; but I could hardly, today, envisage stopping to take it from her.

Immediately after the old bridge comes the vast, tree-planted square in front of the Opera House. No doubt the performance has just finished because a flood of people in dark suits and long dresses begins to pour as one from the three large doors at the top of the steps, exactly as if they had all run out with the sole aim of seeing me pass. Soon I am in the wide road, empty at this hour, that runs along the sea front, driving fast in the direction of the derelict factory where I plan to get rid of my false captive by throwing her into the water at the end of the covered landing-stage, having first taken the precaution of tying her hands behind her back to make sure she cannot swim.

Is it the abnormal engine noise—by now most disturbing—that makes me change my mind? At any rate, as I am passing the ruins of the old de luxe hotel, the gaping embrasures of the ground-floor windows (easily reached from the terraces by stepping over the railings of the little balconies) give me a fresh idea that seems to me better without my being able to explain quite why: I shall deposit my delightful burden in one of the rooms, where I shall have all the time . . .

A bright pinpoint of pain in the fat of my right arm as I am watching the road in the rear-view mirror causes me to lose . . . Yes, it did feel like an injection . . . A dim awareness of my third mistake just reaches the surface of my mind (a second syringe hidden in the thigh part of one of the white-kid boots) before I . . .

And it starts all over again: the muffled tramp of feet in the corridor, the sound of the judas slamming, the silence and the long, deserted beach, the stone falling, etc.

Immediately afterwards the questioning resumes. There are usually two interrogators, difficult to tell apart. They stand side by side. They never alter their position. As far as I am aware they keep their long black coats severely buttoned the whole time and their bowler hats pressed well down on their heads. They speak in turn to ask the questions, but they communicate with each other purely by means of wordless gestures, slow, measured little movements, few in number, involving only one hand, and perhaps the head too, though it is impossible to state this positively because of the very bright spotlights that are arranged in such a way as to blind me every time I try to look at their faces. One of them seems to be holding the curved handle of an umbrella, which he uses to strike the floor with what must be a metal tip every time he wishes to interrupt me.

In order for the alleged trapped student to have concealed a syringe against her thigh beneath the supple leather of a high boot, she would have had actually to be wearing this type of footwear. But the white boots made only a very belated appearance in your system of defence: throughout the early part of the text you were speaking on the contrary of a high-heeled shoe, which is rather different. Do you remember the passage?

Of course! The point is quite right and I remember it very well; the answer seems to me easy, however, because at that stage it was a question of the drowned girl with the fair hair floating like seaweed, one of whose shoes the big bird trained for hunting—according to the legend alluded to—found at the foot of the cliff with its heel broken.

Are you quite sure it is a bird that is involved here and not a large fish? A kind of salmon, for instance, that salvaged the sacred object from the sea and brought it to the shore?

No. If the word "salmon" was mentioned it can only have been to evoke the flesh colour of the rose that has been mentioned several times. And the only fish involved would be the girl herself when the sailors brought her to the surface, caught in their nets.

And yet the factory by the sea, which you admit was the place you were heading for, does happen to be a cannery, does it not?

I don't know . . . And in any case it's derelict, as I was careful to state at the outset.

Let's come back to this question of the tables, not the long, rectangular table on which you placed your victim in an empty room of the ruined hotel but the cast-iron pedestal table . . . or rather tables standing in rows on the terrace of the Café Maximilian. It is not clear from your account—despite a surfeit of detail regarding many less important points—whether the white-coated waiter placed your drink on the student's table or on the one you were sitting at yourself.

Neither. He put the cup of coffee and the little basket of brioches down on a third table a little farther back, which together with the first two formed a sort of isosceles triangle, or even what almost amounted to . . . (Violent sound of the umbrella stick striking the floor several times, its iron tip beating out a jerky rhythm.)

Is that why you neglected to take the black notebook with you?

What notebook? I don't know what you're talking about.

That sort of register in which the false student was

writing her own account as she went along, the contents of which you seem to be quite familiar with, despite what you are saying at present; the very sentence in which you describe the layout of the tables proves it yet again. On the other hand you start by claiming that the girl had not even touched her drink (since the little bottle that stood on the table—but could not have been brought by the waiter—was still full at the time you intervened), and you go on to imply that this was an antidote, taken in anticipation of the attempt at conditioning by intramuscular injection that you perpetrated on her a short while later. How could this alleged counter-poison have done its job if your patient had not even had time to drink it? Let us take things in order and begin at the beginning: what shape are these tables, exactly?

They're round—I mean they have a circular top—with a central foot mounted on a very heavy triangular support (equilateral). Anyway, they've already been described in the report, as have the square tablecloths held in place by four metal clips against the frequent gusts of wind that sweep the beach.

Why do you never mention the apple that the girl was eating?

Yes, that's true, there's an apple too. It's one of the exhibits in the case, each of which occupies one of the listening rooms that line the whole length of the corridor. I don't know whether or not the acoustical soundings have revealed the presence of the suspected message inside. In any case it was not the student who had this large apple in her hand, taking a bite out of it from time to time with her small white teeth, close-set between laughing lips: this last epithet in particular would hardly fit the inscrutable bearing described as being hers. No, this would probably have been the girl in the bathing-costume who was all golden—body and hair—and who was playing ball with two companions in the midst of the crowd when a brief tornado suddenly buffeted the long beach from end to end, picking up wrapping-papers, newspapers, tablecloths, students' notebooks, and light articles of clothing left on the beach by swimmers and whirling them several metres into the air, even tearing up tents and sunshades here and there, carrying off towards the suddenly stormy water an unlikely collection of debris—cardboard boxes, flat bits of wood, children's games all in pieces, foliage from elsewhere—that mingles in the white and blue of the sky with the great sea-birds, which themselves look as if they have been torn to ribbons by the wind . . .

This probably unexpected reappearance of the phantom bird would provide me with a possible bridge towards a similar storm that once accompanied the birth of the idol on the ship of sacrifice. But I am afraid of losing the thread of my narrative if the course of events concerning the apple with the message, the foreseeable consequences of which ought normally to lead to the factory that used before it was abandoned to produce tins of some large fish in piquant sauce, if the events—as I was saying—concerning the apple are not rehearsed without delay: so there I am, sitting in my comfortable cane armchair, on the beach, only a matter of metres from where the water keeps dying away in imperceptible little hissing, silent waves up a very slight slope of wet sand, successive advances and retreats leaving changing festoons of white foam like lines of bubbles in truncated arcs that vanish instantly. This motion of the waves, however, and the tiny fragments of algae and shell that they are today rolling to and fro, this lulling, bring me back to two indispensable remarks relating to the idol, which I am afraid of subsequently forgetting if I do not make a note of them in passing: among the objects carried out to sea by the foregoing gust of wind there was—originating from some open-air game—a turned wooden pin about thirty-five centimetres high and a thin sheet of plywood cut out in the shape of a female silhouette of approximately the size of a real girl; second point: the hurricane was of such violence that it may very well have carried off even more solid items such as the woman's high-heeled shoe, which would thus have disappeared out to sea in a matter of seconds.

But I resume. Settled comfortably in my cane armchair, I look a little like an angler who has cast his line out and is waiting for a good bite, holding in a firm grasp—instead of the flexible rod rising towards the skyline—this slender invalid's stick (already described), the tip of which I am using, with a pretence of absent-mindedness, to strike some hard object . . . I've forgotten what . . . a shapeless, unidentifiable piece of refuse left there by the storm, which was powerful enough without any doubt to have blown away the large, light, salmon-pink ball bouncing without a moment's pause, describing a moving triangle subject to constant deformation, between the three players with the graceful bodies (one in particular—as I said—is remarkable) and lifted it so high in the sky that it would now be floating above our heads, an airship keeping watch on the shore, it too now captive and fitted with a nacelle, motionless as a vulture, observing through a telescope the elusive prey that I have designs on myself, biding my time, not taking my eyes off the lithe torso despite its brisk and unpredictable changes of position as it bends to right and left, then backwards all of a sudden in a curving leap that arches the abdomen, depending on the assumed—or alleged, or even feigned—requirements of the game in progress.

At the same time the young virgin is holding in her left palm, gripped between thumb and little finger, an apple into which she has not yet bitten and which seems to hinder her hardly at all in catching the ball with both hands, as though on the contrary it were a source of extra pleasure to her, stemming if not from the exercise of skill at least from this public demonstration of it. Obviously it would be easy enough to entice her on some pretext or other into the shop with the secret back room, for example by announcing that her prowess has just won her first place in a beach contest, this prestigious victory giving her the right to a made-to-measure wedding-dress, or rather by offering her, with all sorts of specious assurances, the job of posing for some fashion photographs to appear in a well-known magazine, introducing a new model. In either case the final scene is the same, as is its setting: the trying-on cubicle with the secret exit, where an adjustment to a tuck below the hip enables the ostensibly clumsy person performing the operation to plunge a specially prepared dressmaker's pin into the top of the buttock, this time with a single movement; the implement in question is of course a hollow needle that discharges beneath the tender skin the powerful narcotic contained in the little red bulb serving as the pinhead, which need only be squeezed smartly between thumb and forefinger to expel the poison. The victim immediately crumples in my arms, and to signal for her to be taken out the other side towards the cruel fate reserved for young goddesses I have only to strike three sharp blows, using a coded rhythm, with the tip of my stick on the . . . (It's the interrogator, interrupting me again.)

You mentioned algae and shell a moment ago. What exactly were you referring to?

The algae—according to what has been reported, even

repeated several times—are a metaphor for the long tresses, warm-blond with amber highlights, stirring gently in the swell between the rocks against the blue-green of the deep water. As for the shell, that must be a kind of cowrie, the inside of which is bright pink and the aperture a narrow slit with toothed edges. The overall shape is oval, with the upper part convex; sometimes rays of varying length and sinuosity flare out all around the slit. The object is too familiar to necessitate further description.

Is there a connection (and if so of what kind) between this representation and the sponge, the lemon, the little jug, etc.?

An obvious connection! And of a sacrificial kind, without the slightest hesitation being possible. The sponge soaked in acid is inserted in the aperture of the shell . . . You are surely familiar with the effect that lemon juice has on the flesh of the oyster and the way in which the delicate membranous skirts retract as a result of the burning.

Was it this phenomenon you were alluding to when you mentioned the word "brazier" in your description of the evening at the Opera House?

This phenomenon, if you like, as well as several others of the same type, all having more or less directly to do with the consecration of an adolescent idol destined to be an object of worship. The sacrificial slab has figured in the inventory for a long time, as have the phallic toy, the false voyeur's cigar, the candle, the burning wad, etc.

Is the virginity of the subject indispensable?

In theory, yes. But with choice novices, captured without prior examination, it sometimes happens that earlier faults are passed over in silence (provided they have not left any too-visible traces), though they must be

51

atoned for subsequently by additional humiliations and cruelties in the course of special expiation ceremonies. When on the other hand a prisoner is discharged, for whatever reason, she is delivered to the cannery and sold to the trade, after suitable cutting and preparation, with the label "salmon with spices". You will recognize the tins without difficulty amid the innumerable piles in the supermarkets by the pretty mermaid figure on them. However, if the word "virgin" shocked you just now you can very easily substitute another term to suit yourself: sea nymph, infanta, bride, schoolgirl, etc. But do avoid the expression "doe-limbed damsel", which has already been used somewhere else, if I recollect rightly.

What happens to the ones who are chosen?

That question is dealt with in detail elsewhere in the text. Briefly, they become small minor divinities, worshipped by the faithful in the temple of fantasies and lost recollections, the over-elaborate architecture of which constitutes a sort of gigantic replica of the Opera House, a fact that has often led unscrupulous historians to confuse the two buildings. In the entrance hall, on either side of the great spiral staircase (two full revolutions), stand the two monumental statues of the ancient goddess of pleasure in her double guise: Victorious Vanadis and Vanquished Vanadis. Performances take place nightly, both on the huge central stage and in the very large number of chapels set aside for individual use (or private use, or solitary use, or what you will), the imposing or alternatively secret doors of which succeed one another in identical series from end to end of the semicircular passages as well as of the long straight corridors running right through the upper floors, not to mention the labyrinths occupying the various basements.

Why are the corridors always deserted, whereas the

beach is apparently "deserted" at one point and at another "teeming with people"?

I don't know. In any case it seems to me that the difference is not as clear-cut as it appeared to you. There are occasionally lone strollers walking along right at the water's edge, stooping from time to time to pick up a shell in order to examine it, or smell it, or else gathering round some large object freshly washed up to gaze at it and exchange interminable commentaries on its fate. At moments, too, crowds of people throng the corridors, marking time, halted by some bend or sudden narrowing . . . These are men with big hobnailed boots, soldiers maybe . . .

When you said the twin Vanessa eats the firebird at the end of the show, what did you mean?

It's probably another sexual metaphor, like all the rest. If the passage seems to you unnecessary, all you have to do is cut it out, although it represents an interesting inversion of a previous episode: that of the tinned fish. And then you could finish the report yourself if you think you can do better than I.

Are you tired?

Yes, a bit, inevitably: every day repeating these same old stories . . . for nothing . . . But I still wanted to mention some of the ritual scenes enacted in the palace at night, for instance the one listed as "The Fair Captive", whose ankles are attached by heavy chains to iron balls, and also the pink crucifixion with the sponge already spoken of . . . already spoken of . . . already spoken of . . . or perhaps even the tableau of the bride stripped bare on a machine, which comes after this beginning that was certainly reported above: the photograph on the red-and-black prie-dieu, hands bound by a rosary, the hat pins, etc. Old phantoms . . . Old phantoms . . . And still the

53

interminable succession of doors, which seem to have further increased in number since the last time . . . The most urgent course, given the circumstances (fading memory, the constant tapping of the stick, the threatening weather, etc.), the most effective course now seems to me to be to go back to the powerful smell of algae in those corridors. I have always wondered whether it came from the greenish paint on the walls or from somewhere else: the fatigue jackets, for example, whose persistent presence again surrounds me, or the belts, ammunition pouches, and webbing, or the boots themselves . . . Once again there is the confused rush, the commotion, the banging inside the skull, like a hammering in an accelerating rhythm, swelling in intensity to an uproar.

And then, abruptly, nothing more . . . except the faint, gentle, crystalline, barely perceptible sound of isolated drops after the rain, draining through the cracks in the wrecked building to form small, blackish pools here and there in which the rubber soles slide with a hiss. A little farther on a fire burns in the darkness, the crackling of the flames blending with the pattering of the rain on the tin roof, one of those fires that demolition crews light to get rid of a few unwanted planks or boxes and be able afterwards to use the embers to cook their meagre repast of potatoes or fish.

And then it would be morning once again and the trembling of things in the white light of waking. A sleep too short, too disturbed, fragmented by endless interruptions . . . I have a vague recollection of coming in very late, or even at dawn, when the sky is already bright and yet the first windows are lighting up in the silhouettes of the few buildings still standing in this landscape of waste ground, derelict sites, and ruins, looming like scattered rocks on a beach with their four or five disproportionate storeys of formerly opulent residential accommodation, the harmoniously aligned façades of which once formed avenues, side-streets, and squares. At its centre the explosion even destroyed the roadway, leaving a crater that was soon filled by the water flowing from the broken mains; this gutted area, oblong in shape, which had been more or less levelled by the clearance crews, subsequently turned bit by bit into a country lane, too wide, lost, uncertain, winding between the rubble-strewn plots. At this point the black notebook includes several pages of calculations concerning the relative positions of the buildings that were spared—by a miracle, or by chance, or by deliberate skill—as well as a dimensioned drawing of an object with no apparent significance, resembling an egg split along its axis, or it might be an apricot.

The sun would be out this morning, then, and I should be installed with no stick and no moustache on the terrace of the Café Rudolph on the sea-front, having exchanged my dark overcoat and felt hat for a very summery white suit that is more in keeping with the time and place and will therefore make it easier for me to pass unnoticed among the strollers, watching like them, and without a thought in my head, the lively antics of the pretty girls on the as yet deserted beach (why not?) when presently they arrive for their swim in twos and threes and whole parties, running along hand in hand and calling like gulls.

But I wish to take advantage of this moment's respite

55

to read with care the article that ought as every day to figure in the final edition of *The Globe*, a copy of which I have just purchased from the nearby news-stand. No sooner have I opened the paper at the sex-crimes page than I feel a flush come to my cheeks at seeing, spread over three columns, the photograph of the false doctor's little leather case. I had completely forgotten this object, which now reappears—as should have been expected—just as everything seemed to be sorted out at last in an almost satisfactory if not perfect manner.

I ought to have been on my guard, though, when it came to that idle discussion about the supposed virginity of the missing girls. What might such a case contain? Not apples, obviously! Nor sandwiches for the journey (filled with chloroform, presumably!). But I am wrong to laugh: unless I'm careful I shall soon find this sandwich business, which is pretty pointless, coming home to roost just when I am least expecting it. The doctor, on the other hand, will have been recognized without difficulty, even though the passage dealing with him has disappeared from the report for a reason as yet unexplained: this is certainly the character encountered right at the start of the investigation in the long corridor of the hydropathic. After we had passed each other, having exchanged a brief, anonymous greeting as we did so, I glanced back at him without thinking and discovered to my surprise that he too had turned round and had even come to a halt in order to scrutinize me more at his leisure. Possibly some detail missing from his own account had suddenly come back to him? I likewise stopped dead, my body frozen in that awkward twisted posture (one shoulder hidden) that had not been meant to last more than a few seconds, as a movement, but that was now in danger of lasting for ever if I could not find a pretext for ending it. And we did indeed remain in that position, not saying a word, for appreciably too long.

Then he asked me in what seemed to me an affectedly pleasant voice whether I wanted anything. I replied that I was looking for a way out. He did not appear to understand the meaning of my remark, simple though this was, and he continued to gaze at me in silence from behind his close-set steel-rimmed spectacles with what seemed to me astonishment or even solicitude: it was as if he was worried about me, puzzled as to what fate held in store for me, or in some way preoccupied by a question concerning me; probably he would have liked to be of some service to me, had he been able. In the middle of his motionless, silent misgivings he suddenly moved, as if the possibility of a solution had occurred to him at last: using his free hand, he unbuttoned his black coat, then his jacket, and pulled from the little pocket of his waistcoat a large, old-fashioned watch on a gold chain. But what he then discovered, on consulting the dial with a brief glance, no doubt made him immediately abandon the plan that had just taken shape in his mind, because he made an abrupt about-turn; putting the watch back in his pocket and setting off again at a brisk stride, he moved away towards the far end of the interminable corridor. Or else the gesture, together with the easy alibi of the time, served no other purpose than that of plausibly interrupting our awkward tête-à-tête.

And yet I thought at the time that the man must quite simply be one of the members of the orchestra on the way to his dressing-room, and that he might very well be afraid of being late for the beginning of the rehearsal; so the black-leather case contained a wind instrument of some sort, probably dismantled. In fact one could already hear in the distance the intermittent sounds of a large formation tuning up: flute scales or horn calls against a shifting background of muted strings and percussion, while at regular intervals a soprano voice repeats the same short fragment of the singer's great aria. I thus have no trouble in identifying the opera being performed this evening in the great Italianate auditorium of the Casino. It is called *The Golden Fleece*, but despite its title all it is is yet another new version of the myth of the burning bird, which confirms my suspicions regarding the real drama brewing up behind the scenes. Nevertheless it is hard for me now to go on my own way from room to room in search of the one with the wide-open window overlooking the rocks, the sand, and the sea. A wooden, straw-bottomed chair, standing right beside me though I had not noticed it before, happens to supply the face-saver I was searching for: I sit down on it naturally with the intention of giving the situation some sober thought.

It was only then that I noticed the blood, a broad band of red liquid flowing thick and shiny out of the gap of approximately half a centimetre between the floor and the closed door of one of the nearby rooms and across to the middle of the passage to terminate very soon in a little pool of irregular outline, the presence of which reveals a slight depression in the floor at this point that would have been hardly noticeable otherwise. A woman's shoe of fine white leather decorated with probably artificial gemstones has its high heel lying sideways and partially immersed in this puddle of viscous, deep-vermilion fluid. Such a shoe must have gone—together, perhaps, with a tiny strass bag and a tiara—with a particularly provocative evening gown of the kind seen at important first nights at the Opera House.

A little higher up, a metre and a half from the floor, the man's arm that has just dropped this shoe through the open judas (unknown to me?) slowly withdraws and the little moving leaf swings on its hinges and slams shut, leaving the field clear for a further transformation—consecutive but less obtrusive—to take place: the horizontal slats of the blind pivoting gradually on their axes to reveal, in the gap of darkness between the middle pair, two staring eyes.

Then the flat, impersonal voice, sounding like a machine for imitating speech, says: Resume reading. I re-open the black notebook and continue from where I left off: this is the passage in which the masked criminal returns, holding a rose, to the three-quarters destroyed city with the intention of recovering the precious case left behind on the premises. But he no longer remembers either where the flower came from or what he was to have done with it. He eventually throws it into the river, which floodwater has rendered unrecognizable, over the granite balustrade of the old bridge. A large bird passes slowly overhead, flying upstream in the direction from which the muddy water is washing down an odd assortment of flotsam.

A little farther on the man picks up a black stone, apparently of volcanic origin, marked by two small depressions rather like a pair of eyes linked by a shiny groove, lighter in colour, in the shape of a V. The whole resembles the pattern on the head of a cobra, or a sort of scar left in the flesh by a deep gash shaped like a shark's jaw. As for the male hand holding out the object as the photograph was taken, that probably belonged to a policeman or to some prison-service employee.

Apart from this stone, which fell from no one knows where, no fresh element that might have furthered the progress of the investigation has come to light in the past twenty-four hours. I close the newspaper and, without hesitating further, decide to leave my hiding-place: still the same tiny, comfortless room tucked away in a quarter that its last inhabitants are deserting, where an obsolete disguise enables me to present (to whom?) that modest, reassuring, retired-murderer look for which I am known. It's a quiet little life with no problems between the stove that smokes and the ever-open window that looks out on a landscape becoming daily less coherent . . . But what am I saying? And to whom? . . . All questions not worth asking from now on. Once more the hunt resumes. Already, down at the end of the long passage, shut in a last room behind parallel vertical bars, motionless, the lovely and still very new prisoner is inexplicably smiling at me from her cage. Then the image recurs of the iron bed half buried in the wet sand on the long, deserted beach, right at the edge of the little waves. Something—I don't know what—is moving to and fro, borne by the foam. Something once again drives me outside myself in search of pleasure.

Here, then, is what happens on that memorable evening. It is important to give as precise an account of it as possible at this point and not allow oneself, henceforth, to become burdened by details that are either pointless or causally unrelated to the whole. I went out fairly early, that is to say just before nightfall. Dressed for the occasion in a long black single-breasted coat cut straight in the classic style and closed tightly down the front (along its vertical axis) with five dark, imitation-tortoiseshell buttons, a stiff-brimmed felt hat on my head and holding in my (gloved) left hand the little flat case of black synthetic leather marked in the middle of the lid, in large gilt letters accompanied by Gothic flourishes, with the initials W.M. (William Morgan), I had rounded off my severely medical look with a pair of small steel-framed spectacles. Right at the bottom of the three imitation-granite steps—of which on the left only two remain, so steeply does the street slope—I notice a woman's shoe, once splendid but now in a very sorry state, abandoned on the cast-iron grating round the nearest tree. Nothing to be faulted so far.

Predictably this object puts me in mind of the sweet Angelica, whose long fair hair . . . But I dismiss these still glowing recollections, not wishing to stray from my path in order to plunge into considerations that might make me lose sight of my purpose. I make my planned detour none the less via the fashion boutique with the double-exit trying-on cubicles to check that everything is in place. The young brides and communicants in their immaculate tulle dresses are still smiling with the same air of innocence—tender ewes awaiting the sacrificial knife—figures or costumes whose freshness comes as a surprise in the landscape of demolitions and ruins dominated by this small and apparently intact building in dubious Directoire style.

Still on foot since, all things considered, the distances between these three points are so short (this is hard to believe initially), I reach the hydropathic around ten to eight and proceed immediately to the Casino Theatre, which is a blaze of lights for the big première. Inside I am surprised to see so many people already there. In the long corridor leading to the performers' dressing-rooms, to which in theory the public has no access, I come across

61

Franck V. Francis (real name, Francis Lever), who addresses certain incoherent remarks to me as we pass; I do not even attempt to make the slightest sense of them since their sole purpose—quite obviously—is to divert my suspicions. To set his own at rest I play up to him; and we part with what might be an exchange of conspiratorial winks.

At the entrance to the main foyer it is young Vanessa, a second-year student anaesthetist, who next accosts me. The uniform tan of her face and shoulders, which are of a beautiful coppery hue, suggests a better attendance record on the beaches than in the operating theatres. Her brown tresses are enhanced at night by bluish highlights. But the crowd has swiftly become so dense here, the lights sparkle with such dazzling brightness in the faceted mirrors, on the gilt panelling, in the crystal chandeliers, and the sound of countless cheerful conversations, amplified by reverberation, reaches such a pitch of intensity and confusion, punctuated now and then by exclamations in celebration of some unexpected encounter or by the ringing laughter of women in plunging necklines, jewels, silks, and spangles, that I have difficulty in following what the girl is saying to me. Is it apprehension concerning what is about to happen? Or has the glass of champagne that I drank at the bar just now gone to my head a little? Vanessa, for a reason that I don't entirely grasp, starts telling me the story of the death of King Charles-Boris, known as Boris Bluebeard:

He is seated in his favourite chair, the straight back of which holds his tall body upright, in the centre of one of the large, deserted drawing-rooms looking out over the back garden. He is looking at the tops of the hundred-year-old ash trees, leafless as yet, watching the innumerable rooks soaring in the wind above and around their nests. A servant arrives to announce that the rioters are approaching the gates; it is obvious that these are not going to hold them up. The rooks have been making less noise the last few days, fussing about on the edges of their nests, flapping their wings. Probably the eggs have already hatched. Next winter there will be twice as many adult pairs, and their din . . .

But there won't be a next winter. The old king asks how long the revolution will take to reach him. An hour at the most, the servant replies. On the approaches to the deserted palace the regiments of the guard are going over to the insurgents one after another. All right, says the last king, you may leave. He listens to the liveried attendant's footsteps going away, hears the floor creak in the usual places, the heavy door close. He remains motionless for a moment longer, gazing at the tattered black shapes swarming among the treetops.

Then he gets up and goes over to the inlaid mahogany writing-desk occupying the panel between two windows opposite his chair. The piece was badly restored by a cabinet-maker thirty years back. In one of the little drawers beneath the roll-top, namely the top one on the extreme right, there is a tiny glass tube containing three minute splinters of veneer that came away almost immediately and that Charles-Boris has meant ever since to glue back in their exact place. There is an ampoule of wood-glue at the back of the centre drawer among the many erasers, pencils, and penholders of all kinds, most of them not in use. He also needs a lens, a fine sable brush, and a pair of tweezers.

Hardly is this meticulous repair job complete when the armed men burst into the huge room, which because of its size appears to be empty. They stop just inside the door as if something prevented them from going further. Standing ten metres away, facing them, the old king greets them with a happy smile, as a father would the expected arrival of his children to spend Sunday with the family. For a moment the assassins hesitate, so disconcerted are they by this charming manner. To make things easier for them Charles-Boris, nicknamed Boris Bluebeard, assumes the precise facial expression of the four-colour portrait that hangs in all public places and, until this morning, virtually every home in the country, from the humblest to the richest.

Outside, their domesticity disturbed by a quarrel flaring up between rival clans, the rooks suddenly start croaking all together in a fury. Fire, says the leader of the insurgents, a turner known simply by his first name, John, brandishing his stage sword, filched during some pillaging operation, as he gives the order. The aged sovereign, riddled with bullets, sinks to the floor. In the next room the two ex-militiamen's police dogs howl their death-howl.

This last act (which in the programme is subtitled "A Regicide") is a great success, particularly since the music, being both heroic and sentimental, panders to the audience's facile taste. A veritable delirium of applause breaks out. Descending the monumental staircase leading to the square with the first wave of spectators, those in the greatest hurry, I catch a glimpse—as anticipated—of the large black Cadillac moving off, at abnormally high speed for the narrow and intricate streets of the centre of town, in the direction of the sea and the abandoned fish factory with the still-usable jetty. Good: I'm in time. Nor am I surprised when, on the old bridge, I come across the third female character in this affair: the little girl who sells flesh-coloured rosebuds to passers-by and whom the report mentions several times under the name of Temple,

64

which come to that is probably her own. It is she who conveys the secret messages to certain operators passing through, thus ensuring the shifts in meaning at delicate hinge-points in the account.

So I buy a flower from her. Following the agreed procedure, I leave the task of choosing it to the child herself. To ask her to do this I use a coded sentence, which she identifies immediately. Although she does not recognize my face—and with reason—as that of a regular agent of the organization, she suspects nothing and searches right at the bottom of the tray, among roses that seem to me impossible to tell apart, for the one—undoubtedly a fake—that she believes is for me.

To my great surprise (but I am careful to let nothing of it show) it is an apple that she extracts from the mass of leafy, prickly stems, a small green apple that gives every outward appearance of being a real fruit. The little girl offers me the object and murmurs, in the tone of a polite formula at once pleasant and ceremonious, the time at which I am to present myself and the appointed place: the black-painted door, obviously, that has neither number nor bell nor handle of any kind. Immediately on taking the false apple in my hand I am struck by its excessive weight and the extreme hardness of its surface, which a fingernail cannot even dent. Mechanically raising it to my nostrils, I note that it does, however, give off a strong smell of ripe pippin. The short stalk of the fruit, which is rather too thick and stiff, must in fact be the switch for transmitting the ultrasonic signal that automatically opens the black door and gives access to the sanctuary.

As soon as I am inside and the heavy steel panel has shut behind me with a sort of solemn exhalation like the sound of certain nocturnal birds, followed by the simultaneous dull clicking of the multiple bolts of a lock mechanism swimming in oil, I find myself engulfed in a bluish twilight and must wait for several seconds—several minutes, maybe—before I can see clearly enough to make out my surroundings and take my bearings with all requisite prudence.

In fact very little hesitation is possible; there is only one way open to me: a narrow corridor with smooth walls and no lateral openings that I think at first must be long and straight but that abruptly turns left at right angles, afterwards continuing in this new direction, still without doors or adjacent passages; however, it would now be a little less reduced in width . . . A sound in the distant silence resembles solitary notes on a piano, spaced out like drops of water, muffled by the heavy curtains and draperies of an old apartment in which all is motionless and at rest, even the young pupil herself, dozing over her practice in a monotonous eternity.

After several metres, and again quite unpredictably despite the fact that the lighting seems to have improved marginally (or is this just the effect of adjustment?), there is another ninety-degree bend, again to the left, accompanied by a further widening of the passage—for which the word "narrow" is already unsuitable—and probably by a further improvement in the light, too, which has gradually become sufficient to reveal with certainty that there is nothing to be seen here apart from the walls, the ceiling, and the floor, covered with the same white paint, uniform, abstract—one might say—so strongly does it give the impression of being inalterable, offering no hold, proof against time.

Moreover the ambient light, which is blue and milky, poses a further problem to the alert mind of the man moving forward (yet again) with measured tread: although this has increased sensibly, by insensible degrees, it is impossible to detect the presence of any source. Finally an additional ground for unease is provided by the right-angled turns that have multiplied, now to the right and now to the left, though without alternating in any regular way, so many times as to make it impossible to form an idea of the general direction followed since entering the sanctuary.

These various unanswered questions vanish all at once in the face of a new and quite remarkable item of information appearing in the picture after a final right-angled bend: conspicuous on the pale, shiny wall on the left-hand side is a much darker rectangle that by its size and position at first suggests a yawning door embrasure.

In fact one discovers on moving closer that there is no way out here. A virtually invisible pane of glass fills the whole rectangle, lying flush with the polished surface of the wall without any break between them. Beyond the glass is a very dark room, the precise shape and size of which are hard to specify because of the very sombre—possibly black—colour of such limits as it possesses, whether carpeting, paper, or hangings. Only three elements stand out against this inky background, being distinctly better lit or at least, with their lighter colouring, reflecting the light from the corridor to greater effect.

These are, starting from the right foreground and proceeding at an angle towards the back of the field of view, a pair of lady's shoes made of fine blue leather and with very high heels, a long, stiff stem with, at its tip, a flesh-coloured rose like the ones offered to gentlemen in evening dress as they emerge from the Opera House by the little flower-seller known locally by her first name, Temple, and finally the girl herself (apparently) lying in an abandoned position on the dark floor like the other objects mentioned in this inventory.

The little girl is naked except for her long black gloves and a pair of stockings—of a similar shade though more translucent—held at mid-thigh by frilly garters embellished with tiny percale roses. Around her neck is a sort of broad collar made of embroidered lace, also black. She seems to be asleep, but between the splayed fingers of one hand, which she has brought up to her face as if to shield herself from the too-bright light of a lamp (not in the picture), it is conceivable that the child has her eyes open, watching. Or is she dead? Or at least unconscious? The enigmatic character of the whole composition is such, however, as to encourage one to venture a choice, a wager, rather than to join the different compartments together in accordance with the laws of an imaginary organizing principle. So it's a question of plumping for just one of the elements in the picture, but it must be done urgently. The faint, percussive noise is closer now, striking with the curt regularity of a metronome, inexorably.

The narrator, Franck V. Francis, afraid that if he makes a mistake he will find himself back where he started, on the imitation-granite steps in front of the steel door with no number and the handle missing, in the end obviously chooses one of the pale-blue shoes, the one that is lying on its side and seems to have its heel broken at the counter. And immediately he is standing in front of the next window, probably a little farther down the long passage.

This is a rectangle of glass identical to the first, giving on a completely dark space. The spectacle taking place there supplies (provisionally) an explanation for those repeated sounds that seemed to come from a metronome or a piano, or from drops of some liquid echoing in the silence. It is in fact pearls dropping and one after another hitting the exact centre of an oval mirror laid flat on the floor along the axis of the glazed embrasure. There is nothing else visible in the room but the mirror and the succession of silver pearls falling from an invisible ceiling to strike their own image at the same time as the immaterial surface of reflection with a clear, musical sound that is scarcely deadened by the transparent partition, then bouncing up again very high but following trajectories that incline at a greater or lesser angle from the vertical, depending on infinitesimal variations in impact between the two little glistening spheres, which soon disappear together from the view of the spectators immediately on leaving the zone of light emanating from the consulting room, audition room, observation room, showroom, or interrogation room, etc.

The concert continues in a contemplative atmosphere. The note given out varies from pearl to pearl, as does the spacing between consecutive pearls; but it must be possible to identify, amid this apparent confusion, a relatively restricted number of spaces and notes. The question will then re-arise: is one dealing with a problem of choice, as in the previous scene, or is this on the contrary a study in structural organization?

Doubtless plunged in this analysis of the distinct units and their combinations, the ladies of the audience, facing the screen in a semi-circle on seats as varied as they are uncomfortable, lost in their abstracted contemplation, or fascinated by the immemorial cascade of bright dots that rebound one after another in always unforeseen (unforeseeable?) directions, the spectators—as I have said—remain motionless, frozen in highly affected attitudes imitating nature, like those wax figures one sees in museums where famous episodes from history are reproduced in actual size, ostensibly true to life.

Wearing excessive make-up, though in the paler shades apart from the bright red emphasizing the cheekbones, dressed in black and white but in long dresses of outmoded extravagance with a wealth of lace, silk brocade, feathers, spangles, and precious stones, several of them also sport massive rings and enormous brooches, ear-rings, pendants, tiaras, aigrettes, or girandoles of positively pyrotechnic intricacy and apparently made of these same drop-shaped pearls that continue to fall in a vertical series in front of them, immediately reascending to the flies along ever-new parabolic segments.

Others are plastered with artificial roses, lilies, or giant butterflies. Almost all of them have their feet resting in various highly contorted arrangements on cushions, little fur rugs, or lace mats, thus offering as if on a series of display stands a whole collection of footwear for specialist enthusiasts ranging from the ankle boot to the evening shoe and including models with leather straps crisscrossing from the painted toenails to above the ankle. The full evening gowns have in most cases been pulled very high over long, silk-stockinged legs to make it easier to admire the different specimens (is one going to have yet again to back one in particular?), so high, in fact, that at times, in the absence of any undergarments, they expose the delicate brown or golden pubic fleece, carefully combed and itself perhaps decorated with pearl jewellery or little roses, its fissure sometimes revealing still more intimate areas of wax-like flesh if the patient's attitude is such as to keep her thighs open unduly wide.

In the front row, imitating the way in which her neighbour is holding her hands, apparently to stop her ears and shut out the increasingly high-pitched tinkle—

almost a whistling noise—produced by the pearls falling in closer and closer succession, wrists touching under her chin and palms placed against her cheeks on either side, young Temple is herself sullenly watching the episode unfolding in the large rectangular glass where her own reversed image, naked, her black-stockinged legs apart, her face still clasped (as has just been mentioned) in her two tiny hands with their now huge fingers, lies with no shoes on amid a tangle of cushions, surrounded by the roses that have strewn themselves pell-mell from the tray the girl used as a portable stall from which to offer her flowers for customers, overbearing or particular, to choose from.

And it is one of the former sort who has just brutally committed the unexpected assault causing the child to fall with her light load. Behind, slightly in the background, the bald-headed man with the close-set dark glasses can be seen observing with a cruel smile the result of his violations. He may have taken advantage of these to steal the apple with the message hidden beneath the leaves of the bouquet . . . At this moment, however, a stifled cry is heard in the little theatre, though nothing seems to have moved there.

One of the young ladies who are watching the show as if paralysed in their cramped attitudes has suddenly fainted. Without her companions, even those sitting nearest, batting an eyelid, she slumped back with a moan of pain she could no longer suppress, head tilted to one side, lips parted, and eyes closed, unconscious on her straight-backed disciplinary chair. It becomes apparent at this point that she is attached to it; the four serried rows of pearls with metallic highlights forming a dog collar around the base of her neck as well as bracelets around her two wrists are in reality strong bonds fastening the

71

prisoner tightly to her chair: at the top of the upright back and at the ends of the two armrests.

The particularly rigid attitude, allowing no possibility of movement, in which her chains are holding her—may have been holding her for several hours—is doubtless what caused her (fatal?) collapse . . . The more so since the stiletto heel of one of her pink mules with the beaded pompoms has also been nailed to the wooden bar forming the front of the chair seat; this keeps the foot up in mid-air as if in a stirrup, throwing the knee out to one side in a state of extreme flexion and bringing the ankle almost up to the vulva, which the forcing apart of the thighs exposes in full view. Below where the taut suspenders pull into an arch the lower edge of the black wasp-waisted corset that is all she is wearing and on which the lines of force drawing in the waist and thrusting up the breasts are accentuated by further rows of pearls, the red-brown tuft of the sacral triangle is thus displayed with the very greatest ostentation as well as being reflected in the centre of the oval mirror of Venetian glass placed on the floor in front of her by way of a footrest, which is forbidden.

Franck V. Francis abruptly becomes aware of an anomaly that does not fail to disturb him: no one here appears to have noticed his presence. As he cannot have become invisible (even under the magical effect of the green apple!), the only acceptable explanation would be that he is himself a part of the episode: the bald character with the thin-rimmed dark glasses is none other than his own reflection in a side mirror. Contenting himself with this interpretation for the moment, the inspector makes a mental note of the increasingly obvious role played by the pearl beads as an instrument of torture. Several of the pieces of jewellery that they make up must even be presumed to be pinned straight on the young women's skin. Moreover a second young woman is now showing signs of discomfort or distress: crowned with mother-of-pearl headed thorns like a Christian martyr, she is going, once she can no longer maintain the prescribed pose, to drop from her cupped hands—they are chained together with a sort of rosary wound round the joined wrists—the luminous rose symbolizing her virginity, which for her persecutors is an object of additional cruelties.

Meanwhile, on the stage the performance continues: the little flower-seller now wakes up, as if from a dreamless sleep, and immediately begins staring into the eyes of her double, the youngest of the girls sitting watching on the other side of the glass. Without for one moment interrupting this reflective vision, this mirage, she rises to her feet in a pirouette that at the same time sheds from her body the delicate veils of embroidered lace that concealed part of her torso, an improvised chemisette for an under-age prostitute. She then adjusts her black stockings and slips on the elegant high-heeled shoes. Mother-of-pearl butterflies cling to her blond curls . . .

At this last detail the narrator becomes aware of a second inconsistency in the account: according to his recollections, which in this case are fairly precise, Temple, the frail illicit flower-seller of the Opera-House district, was a brunette, a dark brunette. But perhaps these long and softly flowing locks, the colour of ripe wheat, are simply—like many things in this house—a product of artifice? One could swear, for example, that the girl is now even younger, so childish does her figure appear in the glare of the spotlights, whereas the scattered pearls around her have for their part grown in size to become light funfair balloons floating all silvery in the cubic space of the room. At the same time the oval mirror and the

73

strewn roses combine in various decorative shapes of an innocuous nature with no sexual references that can be pin-pointed in particular.

The following tableau, known as "The Bartered Bride", opens with the presentation of bridal wear (full wedding dresses of white, filmy, translucent material, immaculate tulle veils, beaded half-boots, crowns of lilies, tiara bands, etc.) before Temple, still nearly naked but made by the right lighting almost nubile again with her small round breasts, her already pronounced waist, and the incipient fleece shading her pubis with silky down. She stands facing the audience, legs slightly apart, gazing with an air of studious reflection at the elegant couturier-slaves as they lay at her feet the frills and furbelows of the sacrifice. All she is wearing as yet are the long black gloves—one placed on a hip and the other supporting the chin with fingers splayed—and stockings that stop at the top of the thigh in garters, each of which is decorated with a gold-centred rose.

A fresh change in the lighting causes several bird-cages suddenly to emerge from the shadows, cylindrical in shape and of enormous size (the girl would fit in one, crouching), with, inside them, flapping their wings, solitary, possibly starving, great jet-black rooks of impressive wingspan, which thus serve as a reminder at this point (without one knowing the precise reason for this inopportune reference) of the death of the old king, Charles-Boris. But now it is live mannequins filing in gracefully, like brides adorned for the ceremony, the better to show off the items they are presenting. Silently, one after another, the girls come up to greet the new chosen one, haloed by those floating nuptial veils that could once be admired—as has been said—in the windows of the notorious fake shop that played an often essential

74

part in the discreet capture of the many prisoners who fill the palace of mirages.

The girls who come afterwards, led by strict nuns, have nothing on but black fishnet tights, feathers, and their long hair, or again all kinds of profane negligés and intimate light lingerie, the virgin whiteness of which only accentuates its licentious character. One of them, like Salome before Herod, wears nothing but jewellery forming arabesques against her bare skin; another is wearing nothing at all between her soft boots, which just cover the knee, and a plaited-leather dog leash hanging round her neck and down over her belly and between her thighs; several, showing off the perfection of their bare bosoms, have their faces three-parts encircled by those huge and gorgeous aureoles seen on Byzantine saints, where again the pearl decoration leads one to fear (or hope for) the worst as regards the fate in store for them.

But now a figure of death appears in the procession (probably heralded by the birds), she too dressed up in a combination—now suddenly macabre—of white veils and black net. Temple is afraid. She turns round towards the tall baroque mirror standing behind her. Her image seems dim to her and in danger of dissolving. She shuts her eyes. Her awareness of her surroundings immediately begins to blur. She is going to be ill. The water of the mirror tilts and becomes covered with mottling, panther skin, and perforated chlamys; Temple feels herself being sucked up, as into a giant sea anemone, by the now spongy glass and by the floor, which has also lost its consistency, the two having merged into one. She is falling, in a whirl. Her fair hair forms an undulating wake down her back . . .

The little girl finds herself, on the other side of the glass and having pushed back its edges the better to step through the frame, in an immense drawing-room with overdone turn-of-the-century decoration, where a number of motionless young women appear to be waiting for the regulars of the house. Half-undressed (even more in some cases, as if the preceding fashion show had left them only fragments, shreds, or odd bits and pieces), they sit quietly in upholstered armchairs or on couches of dark red velvet or recline on day-beds amid a surfeit of cushions. A few are lying on Persian carpets or animal skins on the floor in more abandoned attitudes, limbs awry, faces flung back, offering their vulvas, indifferent to the absent gaze that rapes them, possibly inanimate. It looks as if certain cruel patrons passing through here have accounted for two or three victims among the inmates. The survivors contemplate the sacrificed corpses without the least sign of emotion, used—it seems—to such exactions.

Meanwhile the rooks have been released from their cages and are perched here and there on the carved cornices of pieces of furniture or the pediments of mirrors. One of them, after a heavy though amazingly silent flight, swoops down on the hospitable belly of a lifeless girl. Another, wanting to be stroked, spreads his imperial plumage, fluffed out in all its splendour, against the bare breasts of a reprieved captive who is half-reclining on a couch. At her feet a lion skin recalls something that must have occurred earlier in the narrative . . . But what? . . . And where?

One of the nuns comes up to Temple and murmurs a few words in her ear, inaudibly, probably to persuade her to join her companions and from now on wait in one of the armchairs in this drawing-room whose youngest adornment she will be. The girl feigns a certain hesitation to hide the fact that she is playing a double game. She then agrees to dress herself up in the traditionally indispensable accoutrements as calculated to appeal to various

76

classes of crank, from the beggar-girl's outfit, or the Christian slave or 1900 bathing-beauty costumes, to the single full-blown rose concealing the vulva.

It is humid and drowsy in the suffocating heat of the trying-on room. Time passes, slowly. It is as if the air were becoming thicker, eventually assuming the brownish colour and consistency of barley syrup. The girl who sells roses illicitly on the street still half-remembers the immense deserted beach, the oarweed with the long wrinkled ribbons trailing behind one over the wet sand, the heavy grey pelicans flying along just above the water, the horses performing caracoles in the waves . . .

She hears, as in a dream, someone reading her the prison regulations: she must do this and that, conduct herself thus . . . the whole meticulous list of directives and interdicts . . . If she is not good she will be shut up in the shop with the dead dolls, where she does not even notice, reflected in the depths of a mirror, the bald head of the narrator.

It is no doubt through carelessness or through an imperceptible miscalculation that I thus find myself shut up again in the prison with the martyred china dolls, St. Blandina, St. Agatha, St. Violet, St. Claudine . . . Yet I ought to have been on my guard from the outset and suspected the trap, my wits sharpened by the corridor twisting and turning at right angles in that over-abrupt way, in other words without the presence of lateral openings (or some other clue) indicating an overall layout that would justify so exceptional a circulation plan inside the building. Anyway, I shall now be able to reflect at my leisure on the risks of my situation as well as on the only reasonable means of getting out of it: the constitution of an unmarred object that in my judges' eyes would be tantamount, if not to my innocence, at least to my non-culpability.

At first I believed the mere description of my cell would constitute an adequate narrative thread. I now think that was a mistake. The wall standing opposite the heavy door with the judas, smooth and white like the other three, is pierced by a small, square embrasure situated so high up and penetrating such a thickness of masonry that the criminal, even from the foot of the door wall, can see nothing but the interior of the wall or to be more precise the top and sides of the horizontal shaft leading, supposedly, to the open air. At this end of the shaft five wrought-iron bars—already described—balk all hope of escape. As pointed out in several previous reports the sounds of the sea, clearly identifiable at certain times of the day or night doubtless corresponding to the high tides, reach the attentive ear despite the narrowness of the passage . . .

I can now clearly hear the shrill cries of the golden-skinned beach girls playing ball down below, under the schistose cliff that, where it sticks out into the sea marking the end of the beaches, is called Black Head on the maps, a steep promontory dominated by the old fort with the legendary past, now, it is said, disused. A little farther on (towards the town) the line of huts begins, their serrated roofs almost completely masking the low dune that replaces the rocks at this point. And here, having just at this moment emerged from one of the narrow grey cells in which she has probably just got dressed, is a tall girl in a long, flowing, filmy white dress who might have stepped out of that famous painting representing Lady G. at the coronation of Christian-Charles, a dress so light that the wind, although without force, lifts the flounced hem well above the incongruously high-heeled blue shoes and the delicate ankles, letting it be seen that the left one is encircled by a slender string of pearls.

The heroine of our recent story, with her old-world charms, has come to rest in the middle of an ambiguous gesture, halted by expectation, or surprise, or hesitation: she is holding one hand out in front of her in the direction of the sea, towards where the leaping girls with the fragile, flesh-pink ball are continuing a game constantly threatened by the wavelets of the rising tide, as if she had meant, for example, to hail one of her companions in order to give her an important message before leaving the beach; but at the same time her anachronistically elegant figure is half-turned to face behind her, possibly as a result of her having become aware of a sudden alteration in the landscape: the upper part of a male silhouette on the dune above the triangular roofs.

Or else this presence, impatiently awaited or on the contrary inopportune, is only assumed by the young lady, who wishes—a very plausible hypothesis—to shout something to her best friend without the risk of being overheard by the man she fears may arrive at any moment. As will have been guessed, this is the man who is to come and collect her in the car, the unfortunate Lord G. in person. He will have judged it simpler to call by the beach himself, since it is on his way, in order to make sure that his wife is home by the time agreed and can thus be ready without rushing and without their being late for the inaugural evening at the Lyric Palace.

The chauffeur, suitably dumb, having closed the car doors in almost perfect silence, climbs back into his seat and sets the car smoothly in motion, subsequently driving along the narrow sandy road without increasing his speed. Inside the large, black, leather-upholstered car the couple do not exchange a word. They are both aware of the dangers of the evening to come, and everything was said between them on this subject long ago.

Since the performance is to be followed by a supper they do not dine but content themselves with a light snack, which they take separately. Lady Caroline, incidentally, because of the sea air and the various exertions of the afternoon, shows far more appetite on this occasion than does her husband, as will be remarked upon without fail by (as well as the narrator) the servants in the kitchen. "The master was worried," they will tell the investigating officers later.

Anyhow, the greater part of the time available is taken up in both cases by the various stages of their toilet, their concern to present a faultless appearance being amply justified not by the tragic end, which they do not know about as yet, but by the special attention that will be bestowed on them by the other dignitaries of the regime, to say nothing of the more anonymous guests at a gala that everything indicates will be exceptional. Unlike his wife, who as usual has a maid, her favourite, assist her, the young lord dresses himself this evening, preferring no one to know that, hidden under his coat in the folds of a red-silk cummerbund, he has a seven millimetre sixty-five automatic pistol, loaded, just in case.

At exactly half past eight they walk together down the flight of stone stairs. The chauffeur is waiting for them at the bottom. Lord G. notices, on the very edge of the last pink-granite step, an offensive object that he identifies almost immediately: an apple core or, to be more exact, the remains of an apple, green in colour, some two-thirds of which has been munched, without the aid of knife or fork. He is about to push aside this incomprehensible piece of refuse, which in addition might cause an accident, with the toe of his patent-leather shoe. However, without knowing why, he refrains from doing so. The chauffeur, after all, is not responsible for the premises being kept tidy, so that such a deviation from normal conduct, in drawing attention to what might be someone's lapse, would in the absence of any other member of the staff be both unseemly and pointless. Stiffly, Lord G. walks on as if he had not seen anything.

But his thoughts are to return repeatedly to the abandoned piece of apple and the improbable glistening green of its skin throughout the first part of the opera, of which moreover he understands nothing. He does not like this aggressive, so-called modern music, and the highly obscure story about a kind of blazing bird that provokes a series of catastrophes on the pretext of coming to the victims' aid strikes him as more fit for the music-hall or the Michelet Circus than for the National Opera House on an official full-dress occasion. Lord G. soon gives up trying to follow the ins and outs of the plot. By great good fortune a procession of dancing-girls in somewhat skimpy pearl costumes arrives to retrieve him from the gloomy thoughts that have come over him anew.

And it is just at this moment that a young woman in a filmy white dress steps dramatically from one of the booths that stand in a row on top of the . . . No, no . . . What am I talking about? Lord G., who had dozed off, wakes with a start and instinctively reaches for his revolver with his right hand. The man on his left in the second row of the state box, surprised by so sudden and inexplicable a movement, half rises in his seat as if preparing to intervene. Lady Caroline, one forearm laid gracefully on the red-velvet trimming of the balustrade, dare not turn towards them. Fortunately the end of this first half of the performance sets the audience applauding at this point and enables everyone to put an acceptable face on the situation.

During the interval Lord G. is surprised to see amidst the brilliantly accoutred crowd thronging the main foyer a very young girl dressed almost in rags and carrying in front of her a tray of roses slung from her slender neck on a length of old frayed rope. He thinks he recognizes the child: it is the one who usually sells her flowers on the steps outside the building. How come she has today been allowed to get as far as the first floor? What is even more curious is that she is engaged in private conversation with Chief Commissioner Duchamp, who scarcely appears to be asking her to account for her presence here or for the inadequacy of her dress: on the contrary he is leaning over the girl with almost anxious attention, listening to the long story she is telling him with an air of innocence embellished with bewitching smiles. But at this very moment a lady in a white dress who has just . . .

"Where was I?" the young lord asks himself, shaking his head in an attempt to put his thoughts back in order. And again it is the obstinate image of the gnawed apple in the poisonous colours that presents itself to his over-wrought mind, as it will also, absurdly, be the last thing he thinks of when, lying where he fell and losing blood at an alarming rate . . . Shouts now go up from all around and in the space of a few seconds reach a deafening climax, which is followed immediately by an abrupt silence, settling as if by magic over the whole length of the beach. All the bodies bronzing themselves in the sun in a variety of postures have sat up, almost in one movement, the few laggards completing their change of position with silent deliberation, like members of a chorus who are slightly behind for an ensemble pose and correct their alignment while drawing as little attention to themselves as possible. And they are all turned towards me, staring at me in horror.

In a last, desperate attempt, pretending not to have noticed anything out of the ordinary, I start to rotate the upper part of my body in order to walk calmly away with as much naturalness as I can still muster, hoping against all reason that no one will dare to intervene. It is then that I catch sight of the young woman in the filmy white dress who has just come out of one of the bathing-huts and has likewise stopped moving, but with her head turned back to face the large black automobile now visible at the top of the dune, which I realize too late is a police car.

She has one arm extended in my direction, and with her white-gloved hand pointing an accusatory forefinger at me in a gesture of inflexible firmness she utters with exaggerated precision, like the actress in a pompous type of theatre playing in a language not her own, these three words repeated three times: "It's him! It's him! It's him!"

So here I am again, chased from my hiding-place, driven out of myself along these corridors that are continually interrupted by unpredictable right-angled turns made even more disagreeable by the successive narrowings of the passage with each change of direction, jostled from smooth surface to blind wall by the trampling pack of black uniforms with their leather-belted tunics to the pallid, cube-shaped, and abruptly silent cell, the three functional poles of which are starting to become clearer to me: first the judas, where two staring eyes appear and disappear between the tilting slats, or which, pivoting on its hinges at irregular intervals, opens wide all of a sudden to admit various objects held out at arm's length before falling—or not—on the resonant floor (engraved boulder, ordinary, clear-glass bottle, thick slice of bread, woman's shoe with the heel torn off, rutilant apple, black notebook . . .), then the interrogations with their dis-connected questions revolving—or not—round these same exhibits, some more, some less deformed with use, and thirdly the mirror-like screen taking up the whole of the rectangular wall opposite the door, which is pierced at eye level by its square judas through which, probably, the projections are beamed also, actual-size fragments of narrative that I have afterwards to give account of. Why afterwards?

But three other, far more pressing questions arise with regard to these images. What is the mechanism organizing their constituent parts? Do they really give a complete illusion of reality? Why did I write "mirror-like"? Moreover it seems to me that, if I could answer just one of these question marks, the other two would then be spontaneously resolved—as in a glass, in fact. I have already described this broken mirror, unframed and insecurely fixed by three loose cramp-irons, that has been allowed, contrary to all custom, to remain on the wall of my prison (the left wall, looking towards the door). It is so high up that I have to climb on the chair (made of turned wood, painted white) in order to catch a glimpse, cut off by the curved and very sharp lower edge, of the upper part of my face down to about the middle of the nose. Make a note of this detail, which is not without importance.

All the other glasses are from now on in the same ruined state on the terraces of the three big sea-front cafés that date from the period of the three assassinated emperors whose names they bear: Maximilian, Rudolph, Christian-Charles. More or less deserted, depending on the time of year, throughout the war against Uruguay, they were subsequently given over to temporary occupation and systematic sacking by the hordes of wild children operating from their nearby dens: disused remnants of coastal fortifications, former cordage works or fish canneries, abandoned bathing establishments with their innumerable rooms for the wealthy guests of bygone days succeeding one another down both sides of interminable corridors in a maze of forks and right-angled turns where, after many detours, one finds oneself brought brusquely back to one's starting-point: blank walls, progressive constriction of the passage, jostling of uniforms, tramping of boots, etc.

And when everything is silent, the very clear sound of drops of water starts again . . . , far-off, crystalline, at quite widely separated intervals that seem to lack the slightest regularity, however complex, each drop giving out a distinct note without it being possible, here either, to identify any kind of law of repetition . . .

Start again, the interrogator says after a long silence, at the broken glass panels round three sides of the terraces of the ruined cafés on Atlantica Avenue. The floorboards being gradually encroached upon by the sand, the tables and chairs abandoned in disorder or stacked in a corner, the empty beer-cans, some more dented than others, that litter the ground, the defaced remains of a circus poster on which . . . etc. So I go on with the story of the beautiful equestrienne in pearly under-garments who, high on her beige horse, spear in hand, has to fight a variety of ferocious animals—bull, lion, crocodile—in front of the thousands of impassive spectators lining the tiers of the ancient amphitheatre. For no apparent reason the investigating officer's voice interrupts me almost immediately:

As far as you are concerned, does the word "rutilant" imply the idea of red?

Certainly.

Thank you, that needed to be clarified.

I fail to see why, but I continue my account without demanding an explanation. The girl is now walking along the immense deserted beach, lost, keeping very close to the scalloped advance of the festoons of wavelets, which periodically wet her bare feet. The lion skin she is dragging behind her leaves a series of discontinuous blood-stained streaks in the damp sand that the sea comes and licks at in places, filling the red furrows to overflowing with its white foam mixed with tiny scraps of seaweed.

And now, between the shifting lines of this edging area, an empty beer-can is washed ashore, to all appearances intact, a perfect cylinder some twelve centimetres in height with, recognizable on it from a distance, the manufacturer's gold trade-mark: a series of concentric ovals, some consisting of a broad black line and the others of words printed in capitals. It would be extremely difficult to determine whether this metal container—about which there is nothing remarkable—really had held beer or whether on the contrary it is one of those false cans, copied to perfection from those of the brewer, that the traffickers use for illicitly transporting their precious white powder, which is discharged nightly at the end of the wharf belonging to the old factory by trawlers ostensibly fitted out for salmon-fishing.

Why did you not mention this traffic earlier?

It has nothing to do with the case before you.

How do you know? All the constituents of the landscape are of necessity interlinked—in many ways, in fact. What happened then?

I went over to the water's edge to pick up the beer-can in order to study it in greater detail. It was during this examination that the shots rang out behind me. I recognized at once the reports of a combat Mauser. A few seconds later the young woman dressed in white came running out of one of the bathing-huts and started yelling. The police car arrived almost immediately. You already know what comes next.

Without the least preliminary sound having indicated any presence whatever beyond the grey door of the cell, the square judas opens wide all of a sudden to admit an arm—a bare arm, visible up to above the elbow, muscular and covered with red-brown hair—that produces a fresh constituent of the narrative.

It takes me a while to understand what I am dealing with this time. The object at first presents itself as a large white pearl balanced on the clenched fist. Eventually I do manage to make out that this is a simple electric light bulb of the ordinary shape, made of pearl glass, the narrowed base and the metal cap being hidden from view, squeezed between the palm and the tightly-closed fingers.

I am suddenly seized by an inexplicable fear, a feeling of immeasurable anguish, at the thought that the hand must now open, as already happened a few moments earlier in the case of the empty beer-can, which fell from a height of one metre fifty, approximately, onto the cement floor of the cell. I still have in my ears the clear, full sound of the

87

initial impact, like a gigantic drop of water, followed immediately by a series of thinner, duller rebounds— sounding like one of those globular bells with a crack in it, or rubbish in a dustbin—growing progressively more muffled. And I can also hear, already, the glass bulb exploding before my very eyes on the precise spot where, earlier, the gilded-metal cylinder fell that eventually rolled over to the closed door, the innumerable white splinters of the fragile sphere now flying in all directions, propelled by identical forces, and creating on the floor—painted a uniform white like the walls—this final image, disturbing in its regularity: a series of concentric rings comparable to those described by a boulder falling from the sky and breaking the surface of a calm stretch of water, the outer corona (made up of the smallest fragments) having as its diameter the exact distance between me and the grey door.

It is like the nine-circle target devised by Chief Commissioner Duchamp, which the crack marksmen use for rifle practice. The beer-can, lying on its side by the door, would thus mark the ninth gradation of this, in other words the one farthest from the centre. Moreover, closer examination of the trade-mark adorning the cylinder of light-weight metal reveals that its oval periphery contains within it a tangential circle or rather one coinciding along almost half its circumference with the curvature of the oval, of which it occupies the entire upper half; this does in fact form the figure 9, which is rendered even more perceptible by a small gap in the line of words printed in capitals that constitutes the lower hoop.

The figure 8, indicating the value of the next circle in towards the centre, is represented by the bit of perished rope, attributed to "the voyeur" in the report, which is at the same time that of the exceedingly beautiful woman welder found hanged among the machines in the canning factory (this looks like flagrant interference with the necessity for crimping the false beer-cans) and the one that the little illicit flower-seller uses round her neck to support the tray full of roses, in which—it will be remembered—the apple with the message was concealed. Did I say that the young worker's name was Angelica? No conclusions have been reached as yet by the inquest that was to have thrown some light on the peculiar circumstances of her death, the criminal nature of which is at any rate beyond doubt, if only on the grounds of the wire binding her wrists together.

I thought, when this thoroughly twisted piece of wire appeared in the cell, brandished at arm's length through the wide-open judas, that here was a bizarre manifestation of attentiveness on the part of my warders: though terribly changed and distorted, this was undoubtedly a rudimentary coathanger of the type found in third-class hotels, thanks to which I was going to be able—after suitable straightening-out operations—to hang my jacket from one of the cramp-irons securing the remains of the broken mirror to the wall. I must now bow to the obvious: the deformations imposed on the object in reality describe the figure 7. I have decided, anyway, to use it to hang on the wall the spoon for my all-too-infrequent meals, tired of seeing this utensil lying about on the floor (in the absence of any furniture other than a wooden chair with no cross-bars) when it is meant to be kept clear of impurities.

Besides, the spoon in question is somewhat awkward for eating with, having at the centre of its concave part a round hole through which I can almost pass my finger, which will make it easier to hang up; however, a small perforation in the end of the handle would have offered the same advantage without the drawbacks of the solution adopted. The fact remains that, in its present state (the handle is also twisted sideways as if a powerful hand had used it as a tool, possibly for escape), this spoon, marking the position on the floor of the sixth circle out from the central point, which is absent, does happen to present to the eye an acceptable image of a 6, somewhat drawn-out.

The next ring bears the imprint of a man's strong hand (the one mentioned in connection with the previous number), obtained in all probability by placing the palm with fingers outstretched in some wet red paint and immediately pressing them against the whitewashed cement surface. The arrangement of this hand in relation to the spoon, which is very close to it, appears to represent an attempt to link the two signs in some meaningful way: for example, the hand could be trying to grasp cutlery lying beyond its reach (since both of them are fixed), which again calls to mind the inadequacy of the meals. The mark of the five fingers, clearly printed in bright red, takes the place—as will have been guessed—of the figure 5.

Is it lack of food? Or the effect of the drugs that they periodically inject into my veins? My head is spinning, my legs giving way beneath me. I would like at least to sit down. But the threat constituted by the glass bulb, still in abeyance but about, at any moment, inexorably, to break into a thousand tiny pieces, paralyzes my whole body. So I have to be content, knowing the same despair as stretches the red hand out towards its holed spoon, with looking at the chair (already named), of which the frame, lying on the floor and viewed from the side, approximates to the figure 4.

Time is getting on. As an entirely natural product of my growing hunger I pass quickly on to the 3 that marks the following circle. This is recognizable without difficulty in the remains of the apple, which has been half munched (as has been said, but where and when?) by a rather narrow jaw, probably Lady Caroline's, that has left two deep notches in the upper part, on either side of the stalk. This apple core is one of the most important exhibits in the case, having been found by Inspector Franck V. Francis in the immediate vicinity of the delicate item of female footwear that had caught by the heel in a tree grating outside the black-painted door with neither handle nor number.

The figure 2 on the penultimate circle is in point of fact indicated by this bright-blue shoe, which is now, here, lying on its side and so showing the straight line of the high stiletto heel, the curve of the sole, and the rounded tip of the upper. Something disturbs me all of a sudden, quite unexpectedly: the cast-iron grating did, according to the report, comprise nine concentric circles linked by intertwined loops, but if the apple gnawed by small, regular teeth really was resting on the third of those circles counting from the trunk of the tree, the broken shoe marked the seventh one and not the second. Moreover, seen in profile like this, it is much more like a figure 7 (the Anglo-Saxon numeral, without a bar), whereas the 2 would require one of those long, curled-up toes not present here, the only peculiarity of the toe of this shoe consisting in a round mirror the width of a half-dollar piece, which is let into the leather and which I had at first taken to be a cut-glass cabochon.

The investigating officers have established that this little glass, which is slightly convex, served the young lady as an unobtrusive rear-view mirror during her delicate spying missions, for example on seaside café terraces, where she was always careful to recline in a deck-chair. Consequently a few minor alterations to the text ought to suffice in order to insert the shoe in the seventh position, where it belongs, in other words between the length of frayed rope relating to the two double agents previously named (the fair Angelica, whose tortured body was used as a lure by the special branches of the police force, and little Temple, the false itinerant flower-seller suspected of having carried the booby trap in her innocent basket of roses, which that evening was unreasonably overloaded, and arrested on the spot to bring to an end the tragic gala performance marking what in the circumstances was a highly controversial re-opening of the Grand Lyric Theatre), between that piece of string—as I was saying—and the paradoxical spoon that I have already decided to hang from the nail belonging to the broken mirror with the sharp curved edge that a careless if not Machiavellian administration has left on the wall of my cell.

As for the twisted wire, that will in fact make a much better 2 than the 7 previously assigned to it, the full, rounded hook of the coat-hanger representing—whereas it has been passed over in silence until now—the upper loop of the figure, to which the horizontal rod designed to take the trousers will supply a lower stroke that is almost in proportion. And the object will easily fall into place behind the apple munched by Lady Caroline, since Inspector Francis used it (unless there has been a mix-up with another, similarly hooked piece of wire) to pull from beneath the cast-iron grating, through one of whose holes it had slipped, the apple core of which the side that was still covered with its polished skin had caught the policeman's eye by virtue of its aggressively green colour.

Since there is no reason to fritter away the precious minutes of the test in tergiversation, those minutes being undoubtedly limited, I stoop in order to effect, rather than go on thinking about it, the permutation envisaged above: the broken coathanger in place of the blue shoe and vice versa. In seven steps and three movements the thing is done.

I must thereby have brought about, more or less unwittingly, one of the combinations favourable to the system, because the situation changes immediately: the arm holding the threatened light-bulb withdraws through the judas in a slow, continuous movement, as if activated by clockwork, and reappears without a noticeable break, this time to offer on the upturned palm of the open hand a large, battery-powered flashlamp. New-looking, nickel-plated, flawless, the appliance also appears to be complete and in good working order; the thumb switch is in the on position and the white-hot filament is giving off a powerful, almost unbearable light through its round pane of glass . . .

A very good thing, too, considering that about ten seconds later the glare that illuminates my cell and that I have not yet managed to trace to any source dims rapidly as if under the effect of a rheostat and goes out altogether in less time than it has taken to write. Without any hesitation I seize hold of the electric torch. This was certainly the right thing to do, as far, at least, as I can tell at the moment, because the arm disappears backwards, still with the same uniform slowness that makes it seem like a mechanical limb, in the beam of light that I have trained on it. And the square judas, operated by an invisible mechanism, shuts with a sharp bang. Then nothing more.

I was expecting the little slats filling its whole central

portion to rotate on their axes as usual, giving a hint, in the semi-darkness of the top slit, or else of the one just below it, of the two staring eyes of a keeper. But nothing of the kind happens this time.

Before long I notice, in the course of examining the door more closely by the direct light of the large portable lamp, that the heavy leaf is not fully closed: the edge that opens is standing several millimetres proud of the fixed jamb, which I have always seen lying exactly flush with it. I move the torch to right and left in order to alter the way its light falls, anxious to make sure that the great novelty of my discovery is not due to the lighting being very different from what I am used to. I have to repeat the experiment several times, with variations, though without managing to make up my mind definitely. That the present arrangement is of long standing seems to me highly improbable, but I cannot say for certain that it is impossible.

Be that as it may, there is nothing else to be attempted but escape. I select with care the spot on the floor where I am going to put down the precious electric lamp, having first extinguished it. When everything is in place I apply the tips of my eight fingers to the projecting edge of the armoured panel, then I pull towards me. The door swings smoothly on its hinges. Before it has emitted the slightest creak it is already far enough ajar for me to pass through. No other sound, whether a swish or a crackle, marks my exit. I find myself, extinguished torch in hand, out in the corridor. After briefly weighing up in my mind whether it would not be best to leave the cell open in order to be able to take refuge there in the event of danger, I choose the opposite solution: to return the leaf to its initial position, which will avoid alerting any patrols.

Plunged, in consequence, into the very deepest darkness

(was there a vague glimmer before, coming from inside the cell?), I venture a few steps in what I believe to be the right direction, namely the one opposed to that which by my calculations leads to the interrogation rooms. But I have scarcely gone five or six metres before I feel completely lost. Hearing nothing suspicious—apart, that is, from the distant, intermittent dripping of water—I light my torch again for a moment by means of a quick to-and-fro push on the control button.

I was able to verify on the instant that I was certainly on the axis of the passage since there was nothing in front of me, but on reflection I am worried about having noticed nothing at the sides either: no lateral surface threw back the least pallor. After a further few metres (perhaps ten or so) I can stand it no longer and press the contact again, at the same time waving the beam from side to side of my path. To my great astonishment I find myself in a kind of gallery that gives the impression of having been hollowed out of the depths of the earth: irregular, partially (and roughly) faced with blackish rubble, shored up in places with poorly squared mine supports, it bears little resemblance—if my recollections are correct—to the corridor leading to the cells, which despite its odd layout had ordinary plastered walls painted a light colour, at least on their upper part. However, not daring to leave my lamp on too long for fear, still, of raising the alarm, I put off a thorough examination of the walls around me until another time.

I move forward in the dark, proceeding carefully with one hand held out in front of me to detect any obstacles. After a stretch that I find difficult to quantify, spatially as well as temporally, my right foot strikes noisily against a very light metal object, which rolls away with a hollow sound after this sharp contact with my shoe. I freeze, ears on the alert for the expected outcome of so untimely a din.

But nothing happens. And after about a minute I venture to illuminate the scene in order to see what sort of thing I have come up against. I should have guessed: it's an empty beer-can, more dented than my kick can possibly have accounted for, its trade-mark almost wholly obscured by a thick layer of earthy dust; the design beneath, which can in fact still be made out at certain points, reminds me of something—even something fairly recent—but what? The floor all around has the uneven look of beaten or rather trodden-down earth; damp, studded with bumps and hollows, it has dark, shallow pools here and there, the residue of some spilt liquid (beer?) unless they are the product of rainwater leaks.

This cavern probably leads nowhere, at any rate to no exit effected in the usual fashion. Possibly, even, no one ever passes through it, has not for a long time, and I run no further risk of making unpleasant encounters. So there is no serious reason why I should extinguish my lamp, especially as the traps, pit props, muddy hollows, or large stones across my path, appear to be multiplying as I go. My attention is caught at this point by a short, light-coloured line, purer in tone, that might be a pencil, a dart, a paintbrush . . . I take two steps and pick the thing up—it's a piece of wood, flat and elongated in shape, which when wiped with a cuff turns out to be a calibrated school ruler of the kind known as a double decimetre. This one is coloured bright yellow and cannot have been in the mud for long because it is neither warped nor has it lost its paint.

Without my understanding why it strikes me forcibly that I must hang onto this object in order to insert it later in a particular place in a pattern from which it is missing, or else to form a number somewhere that this stroke would complete by representing the figure 1 in it, or else . . . It is like a very recent recollection that I can manage neither to bring to the surface nor to dismiss.

But now, with the torch lighting my way, I find fresh reasons for anxiety endlessly presenting themselves to my mind. To begin with there are recent prints in the fresh mud, prints of hands and feet, bare and fairly small as if some youngsters had been walking here on all fours, going in the same direction as myself . . . And immediately gunshots start to ring out at irregular intervals, seemingly quite close though it is difficult to say with any certainty because of these low vaults, which muffle the detonations while at the same time prolonging them with multiple echoes.

There must be at least two gunmen, probably three, positioned close together and aiming in the same direction. As I am trying to reach a more precise estimate of their distance while at the same time proceeding on my way with redoubled caution, I see on the ground in front of me, in the circle of light cast by my lamp, a small high-heeled shoe—size thirty-five, or thirty-six at most—blue in colour but so mud-stained that this is visible, or rather detectable, in only a very few places; the heel is half off, possibly broken during a mad rush across this difficult terrain.

And now, scattered about, come the torn-off limbs and the torso, sliced into several sections, of a wax dummy. Holes with jagged edges, looking as if they were made by bullets, suggest that this disjointed doll has been used as a target for a practice session with combat rifles. Amid the gruesome remains I spot an electric light-bulb, half-buried in the clay but clearly identifiable if only by its holder, which is still trailing a length of double lead loosely twisted on itself; and now, a little farther on, it is on my own flashlamp that I train my beam, or at least on a replica of it, identical in every way in so far as one can appreciate its details, set as it now is in a sort of stony gangue, the only bits showing being one half of the metal cylinder, which is bisected lengthways at an angle, and the flared reflector with its protective glass, all these things here looking as if they consisted of the same reddish matter as the ground itself, from which the object has apparently emerged without managing to detach itself.

I have reached this point in my investigations when the light of the torch in my hand begins to fade abruptly and with such rapidity that I scarcely have time, on looking up, to notice on the wall close by a plane rectangle standing vertically and having approximately the size and shape of a door, at present closed. It is distempered in grey, but beneath the paint one can make out what look like small squares (or trapeziums) of paper, glued one beside another with, in some cases, the edges lifting slightly, describing large concentric circles that fill the entire panel. In places the grey paint is so thin—almost non-existent—that if the light were brighter one would probably be able to see the lines of print on the newspaper from which this unusual wallpapering material was cut with rapid, sweeping snips of the scissors. But the last glimmers still being emitted by my lamp have on the contrary just disappeared, leaving me in total darkness from now on, finally and completely resourceless.

All has been silent since the last shots, after becoming more and more spaced out, tailed off completely. I wait, motionless, not knowing what to do. In desperation I work the slide that activates the switch of my torch to and fro several times, my eyes fixed on the approximate position of the filament. To no effect, of course: I fail to detect the faintest redness. Eventually I throw the useless appliance away at random behind me, myself stubbornly remaining up against this flat surface that seemed to me to be a door.

Indeed, it is one. After an indeterminate period a vague, wan light develops in the vicinity, having appeared so gradually that I should find it impossible to say exactly when the phenomenon came into being. Soon, however, I can no longer shrink from this conclusion: I am still inside my cell, facing my own, closed door, which is painted iron-grey whereas everything else—ceiling, walls, and floor—is a uniform, dull, as it were abstract white. The wooden chair, too, is white. The wire coathanger hooked on the cramp-iron that holds in position the remains of the mirror is as usual painted black . . .

All of a sudden I remember: the hand-print was red, the shoe blue, the ruler yellow . . . Combining the ruler and the shoe would give one the garish green of the apple. There must be some hope of a solution there . . . The ruler and the hand together would give an orange, which must surely appear before long . . . The powerful hand on the delicately made lady's shoe would produce the verb violate, the recall of which very obviously appeared in the length of perished rope coiled back on itself in the form of an 8.

The two staring eyes are at their observation post in the semi-darkness of the corridor beyond the half-open steel slats that form a shutter in the middle of the square judas. Once again I feel the cry welling up in me. I am not sure I can contain it indefinitely. The shrill alarm-clock bell marking the start of the countdown rings out once again. Once again the slats of the shutter slowly and noiselessly close. I take two nervous steps to the right, two to the left, two forwards. I stoop and pick up the empty beer-can. The bolt of the judas snaps, heralding its imminent opening and the presentation of a fresh incriminating object. The numbers, separated by an interval that decreases at each stage, again begin their backward progression, spoken with faultless clarity by the passionless voice of the loudspeaker, the one used for the interrogations ... Nine ... Eight ... Seven ... Closer and closer together as less and less time is left. With all the strength of which I am still capable I hurl the beer-can at the armour-plated panel—right in its centre—which reverberates deep and long and majestically like the bronze door of a cathedral.

Up at the top of the beach, in the bathing-hut where she has just this minute finished getting dressed, Lady Caroline jumps when the metal object strikes violently against the outside of the door. She says to herself: some children are playing football with an old tin can. But the sentence is too serene to reassure her completely, so persistent is her impression of having been taken as a target, if not directly at least through the medium of the thin plank panel, its grey paint flaking off in little diamond shapes, trapeziums, or triangles, that conceals her body, stark naked a matter of seconds ago, from prying eyes and on which someone, after aiming carefully at its centre, has just scored a direct hit with an accurate shot.

Instinctively the young woman casts her eyes about for something that might enable her to resist an attack: a hard object she could use as a defensive weapon or as a projectile. But all she sees, on the wooden shelf above the already broken mirror fixed to one of the side walls of the cell by three cramp-irons, is a large, perfectly spherical orange, soft-skinned and highly coloured, that she has not yet found time to squeeze between her palms in order to make the tartly sweet juice run down into her mouth, what with the many games, sentimental episodes, or minor accidents marking an afternoon that has been exceptionally rich in emotions of all kinds.

Lady Caroline smiles at these still very recent recollections. She says to herself: I asserted my power over the too-pretty Angelica, whose lithe body with its warm-amber curves was drawing the convergent glances of the entire beach as she played ball while munching her apple, all with much graceful flexing of the limbs like a dancing-girl; on our escapade among the rocks I broke the heel of one of my blue shoes; I claimed quite unjustly that it was Angelique's fault, and I forced her to let me have in exchange the ones that, walking barefoot herself, she was holding in her hand; I soiled her dress with red marks without her daring to protest, I looked on shamelessly as she . . .

But here this chain of deliberately trivial thoughts is brusquely interrupted by a fresh sound from outside, more dramatic and also much more dangerous than the first . . . There can be no mistaking the fact that these are shots, fired at very close range from a large-calibre weapon: one . . . two . . . three . . . four detonations, a few seconds apart, followed immediately by a deathly silence falling from end to end of the vast beach, the joyful bustle of which is stilled as if by a spell; and Lady Caroline is again assailed by that causeless feeling of distress that has filled her since this morning with fear of the imminent

101

arrival of an unforeseen, unforeseeable catastrophe, though one already hanging mute and transparent over her, destined to surprise her just when she is least expecting it.

Unable to stand not hearing anything any more, immured in her tiny packing-case prison where the absence of the traditional triangular aperture (occasionally still diamond- or heart-shaped) let into most hut doors at eye level as also of any kind of square judas, with or without a shutter, and even of the tiniest round hole stopped up with a crystal lens (set in the thickness of the wood) to extend its field of view, where this absence—it follows—in any case condemned the young lady to seeing nothing of what was happening outside, she, without further reflection and at the risk of falling into some trap that has been carefully laid for her, snaps back the spring of the bolt with a sharp movement, opens her door wide with a sudden push, emerges into the dazzling sunlight, takes three somewhat unsteady steps in the sparkling sand, and is brought to a halt, with her flowing dress of white muslin all lit up and lending its soft undulations to the sea breeze, her left hand half stretched out in front of her, perhaps in anticipation of a fall, or perhaps rather to protect herself, by the unbearable awfulness of the sight . . .

And suddenly she cries out in the unending silence, a long-drawn-out, manic cry that she could contain no longer. She says to herself: That's it! Now I really am mad. I've finally succumbed to the darting demons of my adolescence, which have always been lurking in the still-water depths of my green eyes with their shimmering irises. On my identity card I am Caroline de Saxe by birth, but my real name is Belzebeth, princess of the blood, more often called the bloody princess. I am walking now down the interminable corridor lined with tortures and murders. Even as a child, right at the back of the attic, where the beams came down too low . . . No, there's no time for that now! This long black car with its windows obscured by thick curtains, its motor ticking over, biding its time, on the grassy road that hugs the dune behind the row of bathing-huts, this I recognize: it's the ambulance from the mental hospital where in a few minutes I shall be back with the sinister Dr. Morgan and his textual experiments, having once again passed through the black door that has neither number nor key and is surmounted by a vertical eye within a triangle of gold fillets, carved point downwards.

For how long have I today (when?) been shut up on my own in this cubical cell—already inventoried in detail several times—where, in the absence of any opening apart from the armour-plated door leading to the special interrogations and so-called clinical treatments along a narrow corridor that repeatedly bends at right angles in one direction or the other without any regularity, so that one can never manage to keep count of the multiple, inexplicable, unavailing detours . . . Where had I got to? . . . "Mistake! Penalty!" announces the cruel voice of the loudspeaker. Then, after a silence, the invisible corrector adds in a more neutral tone: "Go back to: where comma in the absence of any opening . . ."

. . . where, in the absence of any opening, it remains impossible to distinguish day from night. A uniform, wan light of which I have not yet managed to detect the source appears to diffuse from all directions simultaneously, reflected by the white walls, the white ceiling, and also by the floor, itself white like everything else with the sole exception of the armour-plated door, painted a very dark grey, beyond which begins the passage that gives access, after many right-angled turns, to the series of . . .

"Relapse!" shouts the loudspeaker voice, modulating the syllables so curiously that they appear devoid of sense as a result. And then there is silence, punctuated only by the regular (regular?) sound of what I had at first taken to be drops of water falling into a pool, an inmate's wash-basin, an underground cistern, but which turned out on examination to come from this ball, or bullet, or balloon, or pearl continually crossing the cubical interior of the cell in ever-changing directions.

To tell the truth this is an object of doubtful existence, perpetually in movement, too swift and difficult to grasp, on which I at any rate have never succeeded in laying hands, despite my efforts, as if it passed straight through them. Its size is approximately that of a tennis ball, but the material puts one more in mind of those—much smaller ones—used for playing ping-pong: a kind of white celluloid, opalescent, translucent, and very bright, which from a distance one would take for extremely thin glass. So it is not surprising that in a previous passage (if I recollect rightly) this fragile thing should have been confused with an electric light-bulb, and I myself feared initially that it would break on reaching the floor. On the contrary, it bounced easily back up towards the ceiling (in a few seconds reaching a height comparable to that of its point of departure) instead of strewing itself over the surface of the floor in smithereens, forming concentric circles extending as far as the walls, without even suffering the least little dent, as had happened a few moments earlier (when?) to the empty beer-can, which from now on cannot be seen as anything but a provisional, caricatural prefiguration . . .

Oh, my head, my poor, shaven head . . . In short, then, it is this big crystal bubble, this Christmas-tree globule that, each time it touches the ground, emits a limpid, musical sound, the pitch of which no doubt alters imperceptibly with each of its . . . (of its what?), rising perhaps by a few hundredths of a comma from one impact to the next, though without it being possible to confirm this impression with any degree of certainty, even after a period of . . . a period of . . . a period of . . . Once more I attempt—though vainly—to follow the luminous sphere's restless course with my eyes. And now, once more, she is in a great forest of straight, upright boles so tall that their tops are lost in the invisible sky. She is alone. She is eighteen. Her name is Natalie. She can hear barking that seems to be coming towards her, sustained, frenzied barking, probably by very large dogs. There must be three or four of them, possibly more. She takes fright and starts to run with long, lithe, thrusting strides between the parallel tree-trunks looming up on all sides, in front of her too, as far as the eye can see . . .

The barking draws nearer with terrifying rapidity. Turning to look round for a few seconds without slackening speed, she glimpses the three huge beasts with their gleaming black coats and red paws chasing her with all their might, gaining ground with every pace. In her panic Natalie is almost flying, still keeping the same straight course, moving faster than she would ever have believed herself capable of, not even heeding the whippy stems of undergrowth that lash her legs up to high on the thigh where the tender skin is no longer protected, the short cotton dress having ridden up during this wild chase. The barking, more and more raucous now and accompanied by low growling sounds and the steady rumble of the lumbering, headlong gallop, is right on her heels.

She turns round once again. The dogs are less than a

105

metre away. She feels herself weakening. And as the breath from their scarlet throats, now howling louder than ever, brushes her skin with its scalding caress, she starts to scream in terror and distraction. The lead animal, having leapt on her, rips a great flap out of the little dress, exposing the bare hip above the white briefs. The girl tries a sudden side-step to escape. And immediately all three of the ferocious beasts are attacking her from all sides at once, tearing the last shreds of material from her body and biting into the very flesh to get at the skin-tight under-garments, which offer too little hold. Lacerated all ways by the deep gashes made by the sharp canines, her strength exhausted, her courage failing her, Natalie sinks down in the scrub. Her ragged breathing threatens to break off altogether. She is losing consciousness . . .

But it isn't the biggest of the black dogs crushing her like this with straining muscles. It's the hunter now who, leaning towards her face, is half-lying on her parted legs, which means she can no longer close them. His left hand, in its rough leather glove, is holding her by the throat in order to pin to the rubble floor this pretty face with its panting mouth and its upturned blue eyes, lost amid the blond tresses. In his right hand he has the large knife that he is about to plunge into her belly, slowly impaling her through her womanhood in order to finish off his vanquished prey without damaging her further in a stream of vermilion blood. Deep in the man's motionless gaze one can glimpse already the violent pleasure he will take in his crime. Higher still the midday sun, a dazzling ball of white through the treetops, falls on the broad, unsheathed blade with unbearable brightness.

Meanwhile, by dint of staring at it with this kind of exhausting concentration I think I see that this moving ball—which to all appearances is the sole light source in my cell—is not completely spherical but slightly ellipsoidal. There is even a possibility that it is constantly being deformed in the course of its ceaseless trajectory, which would particularly explain the marked change of direction that it undergoes with each of its movements to and fro. Striking the floor with a given deviation from the vertical, it rebounds not in a symmetrical fashion at an equal angle of incidence but, less foreseeably, at an entirely new angle, differing from the first by at least five or six degrees one way or the other, because of this abnormal and variable curvature of the surface at the point of impact; gradually losing momentum, the ball then describes a very pointed parabola, the apex of which—lying almost at the level of the ceiling—corresponds to zero speed allied to a recovery of perfect rotundity. During the ensuing descent, acceleration is resumed at the same time as the bubble stretches, progressively assuming the shape of an egg; it is with this appearance that it strikes the white paint of the floor, travelling at its maximum speed, which is then abruptly reversed (after being reduced to zero in a period of time that has no duration) and immediately starts to decrease once more as the star rises, recovering in the process, by means of imperceptible modifications, the fullness of an ideal sphere, etc.

And this I consider, once again, as it comes back down towards me. What arrow, what knife could put an end to it? I take my poor, hairless head, it too like an egg, in my hands. No, I'm not mad. I'm well aware that that Natalie is someone else: I am Lord G.'s latest wife, Lady Caroline, née de Saxe. I found the story about the girl and the dogs in an old picture book in the attic when I was very young. It also had the ordeal of Blandina, bound naked in a large-mesh net to be delivered up in the arena to the big black bull, whose horns have been specially sharpened in her honour; and that of Angelique, chained to the rock at the foot of the cliff, waiting with no more covering than the wave-borne spume for the giant shark that will come and eat her alive; and that, too, of Griselda, or Brunelda, or Brunetta, a young queen with the very pure lines of a goddess of the ancient world, tied by her feet to the tail of a wild horse that the soldiers, swinging their whips, send off at a gallop through the primordial forest; the victim's dazzling skin lights up all the dark undergrowth, while the huge mass of her flowing hair, cascading out behind her, is like the river in the Garden of Eden. The book was called *Beauties and Beasts*, and I used to think, on the evidence of the youthful grace of those moving heroines of the legendary torments, that it was intended for the edification of little girls of my age, though it struck me as being of distinctly greater interest than the other illustrated publications generally placed at my disposal.

"Now tell the story of little Christine," says the voice from the loudspeaker, falsely neutral and detached though still over-loud, over-present. Although the character of Christine, the communicant, does not occur in the volume in question, I begin none the less without waiting for a second asking, fearing renewed punishments . . . Natalie's body, then, still palpitating though it has meanwhile been carefully washed by the servant women, is placed in a lavish hunting tableau adorning the marble floor of the great hall, among the hinds, the does, the hen pheasants, and the quail. Her elegant curves, her pink skin, her fair hair, all set off by an abandoned pose that the designer has arranged with care, look superb amid the tawny coats and the plumages with their shimmering highlights. The guests of both sexes admire the work of art at their leisure, taking in its sensuality, its subtleties, the balance of masses and colours, not without noting in passing that a little fresh blood is still running out between the girl's parted thighs, adding a touch of a lighter bright red to the crimson wounds of the slaughtered animals all around her. The plan was subsequently to serve up this choice catch as showpiece at the banquet in preparation, but female flesh is more stimulating to the mind than to delicate palates, and since in any case the dogs too must be fed, the girl is without further ado thrown to them still warm, her heart even continuing to beat feebly until she expires altogether.

I realize at this point that the barking of the pack had an excessive quality about it as regards richness of sonority and combinations of sounds: actually it was produced artificially, using the very notes given out by the luminous ball each time it bounces on the floor of the cell. One thinks of the pink-and-white beach ball belonging to Angelica, of whom Natalie's horrible death has naturally put me in mind. Indeed it is her I am observing out of the corner of my eye from the lounge-chair in which I have installed myself on the terrace of the Café Rudolph, which—it will be remembered—is very much closer to the centre of town than our usual beach, lined with its rows of huts stretching as far as the old disused fort.

However, what I am devoting most attention to at the moment is neither the pink beach ball nor the girls playing with it but, with the aid of the little round mirror that does duty as a decorative cabochon on the triangular toe of my shoe, the man in the stylishly cut white suit sitting in a cane chair very much farther back, pretending to read the newspaper held open in front of him whereas he must be keeping a look-out above the shelter of this convenient windbreak, scrutinizing with the expert eye

109

of the dealer the half-naked bathers performing their evolutions as if on a music-hall stage in the strip of fine sand separating the café from the sea.

He has undoubtedly singled out my friend, who in her bright-orange bathing-costume, one-piece but generously cut away everywhere, is zealously doing what it takes to kindle lust. It is Angelique's job in fact, today, to provide the bait for catching in his own trap the most dangerous game of all: the hunter himself, this false doctor whom the organization has had its eye on for several days already and who is said to be one of the suppliers of the *Golden Triangle*, a well-known illicit enterprise of which it has just emerged that Emperor Christian was possibly the most particular customer.

Once I am quite certain that the character's eyes are following my young pupil as she leaps and spins I delay no longer before setting in train the series of operations provided for in the plan. Careful not to sit up (because it is essential that my legs and the upper part of my body remain in a reclining position, otherwise my spy shoe will enable me to scrutinize nothing but the comings and goings of ants or the flight of gulls), I give the agreed signal: lighting a cigarillo. Angelica, who has seen me, immediately gets rid of the beach ball by throwing it to one of her partners—who have not been let into the secret—and starts walking towards us, her dancer's gait now at its most inviting, still holding the green apple in her left hand and taking a bite out of it, in order to complete the picture, just as she sets her bare feet down on the wooden floor of the terrace.

The girl thus passes near my lounge-chair, not even glancing at me, then walks on through the fairly sparse clientele, moving away in my rear-view mirror whereas she is on the contrary getting closer to the man in white as

110

if she were making for the toilet. On reaching the immediate vicinity of his table she pretends all of a sudden to have driven a splinter into her toe, which is not at all surprising in view of the extreme roughness of these gappy, coarse-grained planks. So she executes a series of rapid little hops on her right foot, lifts her left foot in order to take it in her hands, but, hampered by the apple, quickly decides it would be more effective to drop into a semi-kneeling position, as if by chance right up against the false doctor's wicker chair, arching part of her bronzed body—shoulder, nape of the neck, and throat—within reach of the latter's hand on the pretext of examining more closely the upturned sole of her foot.

The man, however, does not flinch, does not say a word. All Angelica can hear is the faint rustle of the pages of his newspaper, which he is no doubt laying down in front of him, searching for what will seem the most anodyne phrase with which to open this crucial conversation . . . But there is no sequel, in this or any other direction. The girl then ventures to look up, prepared herself to seek assistance from this faint-heart if he doesn't make up his mind fairly soon . . .

The slave-merchant doctor is calmly looking at her from behind his steel-rimmed spectacles without a trace of compassion, unsmilingly, as if she were a terracotta statuette in the window of an antique shop. He then lowers his newspaper towards her, having just folded its pages in four the better to display the picture that, without further introduction, he now shows her: "Your photo's in the late edition of *The Globe*," he says.

The provocative pout, scarcely formed, freezes on the charmer's lips. Things are hardly going according to plan; also it's impossible to see what Lady Caroline, on whom the attitude adopted unfortunately involves turning her back, is doing. Moreover Angelica recognizes the photograph, which was taken in the country on her nineteenth birthday, perfectly. Although it is a particularly pretty one of her, she has never given anyone a copy of it because of its private character: Carolina took her bare-breasted. Consequently she can understand neither why nor how this intimate shot has come to occupy prime space in the major evening daily.

"It's the sex-crimes page," the man says, still regarding her with a stern stare. "There must be some mistake," Angelica offers without conviction, not even thinking to get up, so completely has this turn of events caught her off her guard. "That's what they all say!" the investigator replies after a silence, speaking in strange, vaguely suspicious tones. At the end of a quite long pause devoted to some complicated inner meditation he adds, "Stay as you are to avoid drawing attention to us." Only then does the girl become fully aware of the absurdity of her position; she obeys nevertheless, not without wondering quite how her being on her knees in front of this man could in any way help them to pass unnoticed.

"What have you got in your left hand?" The question, put in an inquisitorial manner, scarcely leaves her time to dwell at further length on the previous problem. "You can see: an apple . . ." "Give it to me!" he orders, and she does so without exactly knowing why. But the man, instead of taking the bitten fruit that she holds out to him, leans forward slightly and offers, with a view to taking possession of the object without touching it with his fingers, a spotless handkerchief that he has carefully unfolded in front of her on an outspread hand. Having wrapped up this piece of evidence, still with the same meticulous precautions, he places it in a transparent plastic bag, sealed with a brass strip bearing a row of

112

numbers, which he finally replaces in the jacket pocket from which he drew it a moment ago. "You're going to have some explaining to do about all this," he says in a bored voice, as if sorry for her on account of all the difficulties she has just brought upon herself.

Angelica thinks it is time to react. What will Caroline say if her emissary makes so woeful a showing? But scarcely has she opened her mouth to protest when she is interrupted in commanding tones: "I'm a police inspector," the man says. "You're going to have to follow me to the bureau of special investigations." At the same time he shows her a green-and-yellow official card on which, among other particulars, there appears in larger characters: "Divisional Commissioner F.V. Francis. Vice Squad." So is the young lady on completely the wrong track?

Inside the black Cadillac carrying her off at high speed Angelica tries in vain to clear up this important question. At moments her heart fails her, giving rise to sudden hot flushes, at the thought that she may just have been guilty of an unpardonable lapse: what if this alleged inspector were really the false doctor? In that case she ought under no circumstances to have got into his car. What will happen to her now? The man in the white suit is sitting stiffly erect beside the flat-capped chauffeur. She has been put in the back seat, where she is solidly flanked by two plainclothes policemen wearing very severe black suits and each holding her by one arm above the elbow. They did not even leave her time to put on her beach robe and sandals. She dare not utter another word, surrounded by these four silent and forbidding characters.

The windows of the large car with its deep leather upholstery being masked by thick red curtains, the girl can form no notion either of the direction in which they are travelling as they turn corner after corner or of the districts through which they are passing. The journey seems long to her; but equally they might be driving her round in circles. They arrive by way of an underground garage, which likewise prevents her from registering the external appearance of the building they have entered.

As soon as she has stepped from the car she is unceremoniously pushed along a complicated corridor to a completely white, cube-shaped cell in which the only furniture is a wrought-iron bedstead without either sheets or blankets, nor even a mattress, and a dressing-table in the same style, made of twisted rods of iron, it too painted black. More detailed observations are postponed till another time because the door now opens to admit a man in a white surgeon's coat, accompanied by a nurse. With movements that are quick and firm in the extreme, though devoid of any unnecessary brutality, they lay the prisoner down on the criss-crossed metal slats of the bed, take her pulse, measure her blood pressure, examine her nostrils, her open mouth, the insides of her eyelids. Then, still without a word being spoken, they roll her over onto her front and immediately give her an intramuscular injection in the upper part of her buttock by way of an opening in the bathing-costume that looks as if it was designed specifically for this purpose. The sudden, painful jab induces a brief lumbar spasm.

Angelica is so bewildered by everything that is happening to her that she submits to it as if she had come here of her own free will to undergo this medical examination. Is any other course open to her, in fact? But once her visitors have left the room an additional misgiving crosses her already clouded mind: haven't they just administered some truth serum that is going to make her betray her mistress's confidence? She has a further, vague impression of two staring eyes watching her as she lies on her bed of blackened steel, through the variable gaps between the swivelling slats of the judas; but she is already slipping off to sleep.

It is the two policemen dressed in black who wake her up, with a start. How long has she been asleep? She feels herself being handled like a rag doll and does not even notice, at the time, that they briskly snap a pair of manacles on her wrists in order to fasten her hands together behind her back. She becomes aware of this several seconds later as they drag her from the cell, still barefoot and in her immodest bathing-costume, to lead her at a run along the same narrow corridor with its sudden, innumerable, inexplicable right-angled bends . . .

The interrogation takes place in an immense hall with a high, vaulted, vaguely Gothic ceiling, a floor paved with uneven stones, and pillars as in a church. It is rather cold here, at least for so scanty a costume. The man in the white suit is sitting behind a large and luxurious Directoire-style desk made of mahogany with bronze mounts. It is the only piece of furniture to be seen in the whole enormous room. Angelique has been placed standing in front of her judge. Without having unfastened her hands, the two policemen who led her here subsequently disappeared in the shadows. For the only light, coming from several clusters of spotlights up in the flies, falls on the place where the accused is standing. She can, however, clearly make out the man sitting opposite her, thanks to the white cloth of his jacket and the little lamp that shines on the books and papers spread out on his desk.

After going through certain of these at great length, he finally looks up at his prisoner. The swiftness with which his subordinates, whether warders or doctors, execute

115

every little gesture and shift of position is in contrast to their boss's habit of leaving an abnormally long pause for thought between each of his movements and utterances. This might be the first time he has set eyes on the girl, so prolonged is his inspection of her. Eventually, as if guessing her thoughts, he says simply, "You can't sit down, it's against the rules." And he goes back to his files.

Abruptly his manner changes. In smoothly playful tones he says, looking up with a smile, "If you'd rather kneel, you may, though there's nothing to say you must!" But immediately he recovers his usual ice-cold demeanour, adopting a thoroughly lugubrious intonation to complete his sentence: ". . . in the present case, that is." Angelica bites her lip. She is afraid she will start to cry. She tugs impatiently at her chains, which feel ice-cold in the small of her back and are not at all like the slim handcuffs in use with the police; on the contrary they seem more like heavy, antiquated armbands such as were worn by slaves or convicts, joined by three or four wrought-iron links. This detail suddenly disturbs her more than all the rest.

"I don't understand . . ." she begins; and she goes no further, surprised by the timidity of her own voice, which is almost inaudible. The inspector stares at her curiously. Then he gives a brief, mocking laugh. "Injection," he says, addressing an invisible nurse who, appearing at that moment, perhaps deliberately sticks the needle in too slowly and then empties the syringe too fast; the girl gives a feeble cry of pain and protest. But this reflex action will be her last. She feels her will-power gradually ebbing away. A different type of drug must have been used this time, for why would they put her to sleep here? "A picture of docility," the false inspector concludes.

After continuing to watch the patient closely for almost a minute to make sure she shows no further

116

inclination to resist, he begins speaking in a hard, dry, mechanical voice: "Identification. Simply answer each of my questions with yes, not forgetting to add sir, for form's sake. Your name is Angelica Salomon. Salomon, not Salmon as wrongly indicated on your recent medical sheet."

Then, abruptly, he again changes to a different register, and it is as if lost in a distant reverie that he utters the following sentence: "Salmon . . . Too bad . . . You might have been able to swim without the help of your arms . . ." Angelica, not understanding, replies, "Yes, sir," as to the previous assertions, though in a more uncertain voice. There is a silence. The man stares straight ahead of him, apparently not seeing anything any more. At last he looks down at his notes and resumes in an inquisitorial manner: "You recognized your photograph in last night's *Globe*. You've given up pretending it isn't you."

He looks alternately at the girl and at the sheet of newspaper that he has unfolded in front of him, with or without his spectacles, which he removes and replaces several times to appraise the difference. "Indeed, as far as the face is concerned there's no doubt at all. Let's have a look at the rest." He signals briefly with a hand and one of the policemen steps up to the prisoner, releases the spring of a flick knife, making the thin blade snap out, briskly severs the bathing-costume's only strap, and tugs at the material so roughly with both hands that it tears into three pieces, one of which is ripped away completely and falls to the floor while the two other, smaller pieces are left hanging in shreds over one hip and down between the thighs. Angelica is thus naked down to mid-belly, the rest of the costume only clinging to her skin thanks to the elasticity of the material and to the girl's chained hands,

117

with which she is doing her best to hold up one of the shredded edges behind her back. The man who did it has disappeared as abruptly as he appeared.

Franck V. Francis stares intently at the golden-bronzed bosom, now and again transferring his gaze to the reference photo, this time without taking off his steel-rimmed spectacles. "Good," he says, adding almost immediately, in the same official tone, "You have my congratulations!" He begins writing busily at the bottom of the open page of a large register.

This time taking his cue from a different document, he continues running through the record: "Your body, cast up by the high tide, was found near the middle of the long beach that stretches from the canning works to the disused fort. You had your hands fastened together behind your back . . ." He glances at the person concerned in order to verify this last detail. "Yes, that's right," he says and resumes reading: ". . . with fifty-amp electric cable, non-twisted. However, drowning does not seem to have been the cause of death, which may have occurred some considerable time before. Marks of strangulation (by hanging or otherwise) with a thick rope . . ."

The inspector stops to take a further look at the live object of the report, sees no marks on the neck, and looks back at his papers, which he begins to shuffle feverishly. Eventually he murmurs as if to himself, "No, come on . . . We're not there yet . . ." Then, addressing the girl: "Forgive me, I had the wrong page. I resume: you worked as a welding operative in the old cannery by the seashore. You left that job two months ago to join Lord G.'s private secretariat. You are not surprised at this sudden jump up the social scale, which is all the stranger for the fact that the young lord is an out-and-out homosexual.

118

Or at least was. . . , since (it's no use feigning astonishment) he was murdered in public only last night, while you were pretending to be asleep and we were drawing up your dossier." He closes his notebook with an impatient movement, having completely recovered his self-assurance.

Angelica, frozen like a statue, no longer knows herself what she does know and what she does not. "Final point of the charge," the inspector concludes, giving her a hard stare. "This does not appear in the report as yet, but we shall soon remedy that. You are suspected of having belonged, before you were taken on at the antiquated canned-fish factory, to a band of youths living wild. You know that the extermination order is still in force. And it would be a mistake to believe that your beauty will curb the executioners' zeal. Your magnificent body, fine-textured skin, and indubitably attractive face will on the contrary ensure that your sufferings, and their pleasure, are both prolonged."

These final sentences of his text seem all of a sudden to have wearied Inspector Francis beyond measure. He says, "Right! That's all for this evening." He signals to the two policemen in black: "Take the young lady back to the room. You may violate her if you like. But nothing more for the moment."

In the corridor leading to the cells three gentlemen in evening dress—tail coats, silk scarves, and top hats—no doubt on their way home from the gala re-opening of the Grand Lyric Theatre, pass Angelica with her warders on either side of her, moving aside to make room for them and politely doffing their hats to the girl without showing the least surprise at the pleasing spectacle of her nudity or at the medieval barbarity of her chains. The oldest of them, who could be about fifty, inquires quite naturally

119

of one of the policemen which room she occupies, this detainee whose face he has never seen before. The man addressed answers in a deferential tone: "Not allocated yet, sir. She's undergoing provisional conditioning: her case is being investigated."

"Well, hurry up and convict her," says the man in the dress coat, delicately squeezing between thumb and forefinger, in a fatherly gesture of undeniable benevolence, a nipple that the narrowness of the passage brings within reach of his white-gloved hand. Angelica modestly returns his smile. "And if it's a death sentence to be carried out immediately, do please let me know in time nevertheless. I should like at all events to be present at the execution." The victim-to-be lowers her head a little in confusion as if this were a mark of attention by which she must show herself flattered, to do with some school examination, perhaps in dancing or music.

"Wasn't it her photo in the papers yesterday?" one of the aides accompanying the chief commissioner of police then asks. "Yes," replies the second warder, "in fact that's what made us smell a rat, in a manner of speaking." "Drowned by a sex maniac, they say?" "Our thinking at the moment is rather that she was sacrificed in the course of some religious ceremony." "Ah, very good," the chief commissioner says approvingly. "She's certainly worthy of it." And with this final compliment he bows once more to the stranger and walks off, flanked by his assistants.

As she completes the rest of the short journey with its unexpected bends Angelica wonders why, despite the clarity of mind she feels she has recovered, she is not more frightened by what she has just heard. Actually she had the impression they were talking about someone else. When, the armour-plated door of the white cell once closed, they brutally rip off the shreds of the torn

120

bathing-costume that were still after a fashion shielding her most private charms, she merely casts her eyes down in an entirely natural access of modesty and abandons herself submissively and engagingly to the caresses of the two men in the various attitudes that they make her adopt, though without disencumbering her of her heavy manacles.

Meanwhile the judas opens wide for the issue of the daily meal. Although the gaolers need no longer fear the least rebellion on the part of their docile captive, they take pleasure in making her eat without freeing her hands, obliging her in consequence to grovel in front of her bowl where it has been laid on the floor, in addition spreading her knees as far apart as possible under threat of punishments of extreme cruelty should she soil herself in the process. Fascinated by her suppleness and by the persistent seductiveness of her more constrained postures, they afterwards lead her, in the same get-up, to the toilet, which is of the seatless variety, in order to see her crouch down with thighs apart and then make delightful contorsions in putting the paper to use.

Back in the room, after playing with her for a while longer, she still docile and smiling, they finally fasten her to the iron bed with her long legs quartered. A number of rings and straps are fitted all around it for this type of use. But today they content themselves with attaching her ankles to the two sides of the metal frame, pulling the broad belts of stiff leather tight enough to make the patient flex her knees slightly, so opening up her vagina more widely. Her hands, still chained behind her back, force her in addition to arch her body upwards, which narrows her waist even more and brings out the amphora-like swell of her hips.

At the base of her belly with its silky skin, ever so

slightly paler as are her breasts and the insides of her thighs, the triangular fur of the pubis is the same bright red-blond colour as the tangled mass of curly hair, where beneath stray locks two huge green eyes shine brightly, widened now by fear of being left alone, a prey to drug-induced phantasms.

This is the state in which Dr. Morgan will find her when he enters the experimentation chamber some hours later.

So Dr. Morgan, before going to the laboratory where he conducts his experiments in tertiary dream behaviour, called at G. Court, where he met Chief Commissioner Duchamp for the routine investigation in connection with the dramatic death of the young lord. The presence of the forensic pathologist is in fact a pure formality since the death unfortunately leaves no room for doubt, nor does the precise time it occurred, nor does its immediate cause. But one never knows, says Duchamp with that man-of-the-world half-smile that makes him pass for shrewd and possessed of secret resources.

In any case he gives little credence to the official version of the loathsome crime, despite the victim's dubious morals, a delayed-action bomb of that expensive and sophisticated type in no way forming part of the usual villain's armoury. Questioning of the chauffeur and the three male servants has produced no result, nor has that of the many secretaries, chambermaids, and favourites who fill the vast mansion. All these people, quite understandably, are still distraught as a result of the crime, though not the very young mistress of the house who, for her age, is displaying exceptional coolness.

It is in the small yellow drawing-room, which is decorated with souvenirs of varying degrees of authenticity brought back from Turkey where the couple spent their honeymoon, that she receives visitors. After a certain amount of small talk of a metaphysical and condolatory nature, Duchamp asks abruptly, "What were your precise whereabouts when the explosion occurred?" "My precise whereabouts were the lavatory," replies Lady Caroline with a note of challenge in her voice. The quick smile that passes over the chief commissioner's lips is like a nervous twitch. "And of course," he says, "the noise of the booby-trap reached you there?" "Good heavens, yes!" "How long was it then since you had left your husband?" "About seven minutes." Duchamp considers this, clearly making some nimble yet intricate calculation in his head on conclusion of which he says simply, "One of your prettiest secretaries has disappeared, has she not?"

But the young lady continues to reply without embarrassment: "Yes, I know: Angelica von Salomon." "When was the last time you saw her?" "Early afternoon." "Where was she at that time?" "In the mail room." "You have no idea what she did subsequently?" "No. None." Having spoken these words with finality, she adds almost aggressively, "I don't, however, see the connection."

Duchamp considers her in silence for a moment, then the brief labial contraction that serves him for a smile once again crosses the lower part of his face. "As far as making connections is concerned," he says, "you can leave that to us." After quite a long pause, occupied by thoughts of his own, he resumes: "Have you known this

123

Miss von Salomon long?" "A month and twenty-seven days." "So you had never seen her before you took her onto your secretarial staff?" "I didn't employ her; my husband did. He didn't tell me who had recommended her." Duchamp says nothing for thirty or forty seconds, then, after consulting the still silent Dr. Morgan with a rapid glance, he goes on: "Did her state of mind strike you as leaving nothing to be desired? Or do you think her capable of fugues, whims, attacks of nerves, dissociation, sleepwalking, sudden violent emotions, morbid erotic fantasies, or other things of that sort?"

Lady Caroline does not flinch. She looks the policeman straight in the eye, not batting an eyelid, and says, articulating each syllable, "I fail to understand what you are trying to suggest." But Duchamp is not to be put off so easily. He calmly returns her gaze, then says, after a pause to give his words their full effect, "We found one of the delicate, pale-blue, high-heeled leather shoes that you were wearing on the beach around mid-afternoon. There were blood-stains on the toe. I've just had the result of the analysis: it's neither your own blood nor the late Lord G.'s."

This time the offender has blushed so violently that she is incapable of carrying it off any longer. She immediately decides to accentuate the outward signs of her embarrassment even further: she brings her hands up to her forehead, sketching in the process a few distracted gestures as if to drive away spectres flickering before her pale-blue pupils. "Forgive me," she gasps. "It's been a hard day and I'm exhausted. I'm going to have to retire. Do please call back in the morning if you need to ask me any more questions." "Thank you, madam, but that will probably not be necessary," the chief commissioner replies, rising from his chair and executing a formal bow in her direction without making the slightest allusion to her alleged indisposition. As he is going out through the door he turns to add, "We shall, however, have to come back to take some of your young soubrettes and confidantes away in order to question them more conveniently at the criminal police's special premises."

As soon as she is alone Lady Caroline hurries upstairs to her all-white room, where she throws herself on the thick polar-bear skin coverlet gracing the great brass bed. Although she need not, now, go on play-acting for over-inquisitive spectators, she abandons herself to her distress in the ever-vain hope of making it pass more quickly. She lets her blond head toss from side to side among the cushions, the long hairs of which become mingled with her own tresses, and suddenly she stops still, eyes wide and staring at the angle of the wall beneath the cornice, to say aloud a series of confused syllables recognizable, possibly, as the three words: Angelique's Crimson Curse. Up under the ceiling the little round pearl bulbs of the chandelier, bright and clearly visible among all the crystal pendants, begin to move, slowly at first, then more quickly, tracing co-axial circles. Caroline thinks in terror that she is going to start screaming again.

Dr. Morgan, standing beside the bed, leans a little farther over her and observes her with his cold eyes as if trying to decipher a difficult text, or to hypnotize her. But she braces herself, refusing to submit yet again to his power. She shakes her head desperately in order to break free. She says, "Can't you see I'm burning?" The little points of light are now moving all over the room. She is in the convent chapel, which is lit by the dozen very slender candles that have just been brought in, standing at least a metre high, like needles tipped with fire. She is fifteen. Her name is Christine. Today is her solemn communion.

She is kneeling on a black wooden prie-dieu with a perforated back carved in flames and volutes (like the smoke of incense, or of a martyr's pyre), the padded seat and arm-rest of which are covered with bright-red velvet. The six companions flanking her, three on each side, in line before the row of silver church candlesticks, dressed like her in white tulle and kneeling on low prayer-stools (more rustic, though, made of plain, hard wood), seem much less old than she is: twelve or thirteen at most; one can see by their bodices that they are still children.

Christine cannot quite remember why she herself is late in performing this religious ceremony. Another, more disturbing delay weighs heavier on her mind. But the priest who is to insert the host in their half-open mouths, having first heard the confessions of all seven in public, enters from behind the altar. And whom should she recognize to her horror than Dr. Morgan himself. He says, pushing his stern face close and with his whole massive body looming like a giant above the brass bed that he is about to crush: You have a temperature. We're going to give you an injection to let you sleep. An involuntary movement of rebellion half-raises her on one elbow: No! No! No injections, I beg of you! But she slumps back, her strength exhausted, in the white fur.

Brutally wrenched from a deep sleep in the middle of the night, she thinks she is battling with a nightmare that will not go away; but it really is two officers of the law in black tunics and leather belts dragging her from her bed to take her for questioning. All she is wearing is a young bride's—or whore's—chemisette of transparent pink tulle, full and flounced, that starts only just above her breasts and scarcely reaches below the tip of her pubis. It is like one of those that Caroline took on the Turkey trip

126

when she was still hoping to recall her husband to an allegiance that held no attraction for him. That'll be fine for the road, declare the policemen, who seem to be in a hurry to have done with her.

So it is in this attire, and barefoot, that they fling her into their car, only to leave it again soon afterwards not far from the "Mermaid" brand salmon factory and continue the journey on foot on the pretext of taking a short cut, crossing the bay to the old fort by way of the wide expanse of beach left exposed by a very low tide. The night is bright, the sky almost completely clear, and the full moon makes the wet strand glisten with innumerable flickering highlights, gone in an instant, and with great glossy patches that move along, keeping pace with every step.

The smooth sand is littered with clumps of blackish seaweed, slippery if trodden on so best avoided, but also with large numbers of drowned corpses washed up by the sea, children and youths of both sexes, most of them quite naked and with fresh injuries. Judging by their perfect state of preservation, their deaths can only have been recent and none of them can have been in the water for very long. Huge green crabs, bigger than rats, move from wound to wound, adding variety to their feast.

The two uniformed policemen walk in front, turning round from time to time to shout at the young woman to go faster. But the distance between her and them becomes progressively greater. Sometimes, to wait for her for a moment, they stop near a prostrate form, and it is invariably a boy, whereas the girls are far more numerous. Having just lingered for an instant by the dislocated body of one of these, whose arms and legs are almost completely torn off, she having probably been quartered on some machine, Caroline lifts her eyes to look for her

127

warders. For as far ahead as she can see, there is no one there any more.

Nevertheless she resumes walking, though she has now forgotten where she was going. The moist, warm air of the tropical night is laden with smells: over-ripe fruit or sickly-sweet flowers, mingled with iodine and slime. The pieces of jetsam dotted all over the flat, gleaming strand are like the discarded objects of some old, abandoned story: an apple core, a broken chair, the skeletal framework of a wrought-iron bed. Angelica's pink-and-white beach ball is there too, serving no purpose now, as well as several clear light-bulbs: at least, such is one's first impression on seeing these small, scattered bubbles, all white and shiny; looked at more closely, however, their completely spherical shape, lacking any sort of cap by means of which they could be screwed into a socket, makes that application most unlikely. No, these must in fact be the eggs of some chimera, dredged up from the depths of the ocean by the high tides.

And now Caroline stoops to pick up another piece of rubbish: her second blue shoe, the faceted cabochon of which has been ripped off with a pair of pliers, leaving a wide, open wound in the soft leather extending from the middle to the tip of the triangle that constitutes the front portion of the upper. This forms a kind of mouth, gashing the toe of the shoe along its longitudinal axis. And there is blood flowing from between the two parted lips; the thick liquid, however, looks black in the moon's funereal beams.

In the dawn, once again, my face to the wan, almost horizontal rays of the rising sun, I am walking along the immense, deserted strand, right at the water's edge. The sea is a milky jade-green, the distances tinged with very pale yellow and violet; the tide is in now, and all it leaves uncovered at the foot of the dune with its stiff tufts of grey grasses is a narrow, gently sloping strip of dry sand, evenly dented all over by the romping bathers in daily, elusive attendance, and now gone.

Below the black line formed by tiny fragments of dead algae mixed up with other refuse of more questionable origin that marks the highest point reached by the tide, a uniform surface alternately flooded and exposed by successive little waves in ever-changing festoons makes progress less arduous at times, if still under constant threat, strewn with pitfalls, to say nothing of the big conical or ovoid shellfish with the pearly-pink vulvae—said to be dangerous even to touch—that stand out here and there in the arcs of shiny beach as if on a moving mirror.

And here comes the little beggar-prostitute in her tattered white veils that might once have been some virginal wedding or first-communion dress. In spite—or perhaps because—of the wild radiance of her beauty, a blend of violence and fragility, which with her red-gold hair puts one in mind of a young lioness escaped from a circus, or come down in the night from the nearby forest, men are afraid of her: she is believed to cast spells on those rash enough to take her to their beds; as a result her unstable clientele is recruited mainly among foreigners, the insane, sex maniacs, and murderers. For my part, there is one thing that has been bothering me for a long time: it's always in the same direction that she follows the curving shoreline like this, without her ever being seen to

129

return. Does she do so at dead of night, under cover of the deepest darkness, which only ghosts seek to share with the votaries of drugs and crime? Or does she come back by a secret route, passing through the hinterland by way of dubious suburbs not marked on any map, where temporary huts are dotted in confusion among ruined quarters, derelict sites, and areas of waste ground? It is possible she lives in the underground passages of the old fort, despite the giant scorpions that prevent tramps as well as lovers in search of solitude from venturing inside, or it might be in the luxurious ruins of the hydropathic: all dusty marble and flaking gilt, mirrors punctured with stars or firework patterns by the impact of machine-gun bullets, smashed columns, crumbling balustrades, empty fountain basins, broken statues, rooms with neither windows nor doors and now given over to the seabirds.

Walking faster than she (for in the absence of any onlookers I do not use my stick, which obviously serves no purpose), I have soon caught her up, and my attention is drawn yet again by her curious gait: the foot left behind for a second too long, poised on tiptoe at right angles to the ground, motionless for a moment before taking off, the same fascinating phenomenon recurring identically with every step she takes. All of a sudden the idea flashes through my mind that it would probably be wiser to get rid of this possible witness to my presence so early in the morning in a place so little frequented at such an hour . . .

But whom would she tell? And why? And who would place the slightest credence in the evidence of a half-mad girl who was a witch into the bargain, suspected of the direst misdeeds? Then, on second thoughts, having long ago passed her whereas her foot in that vertical position remains present in my retinal memory, I tell myself it was perhaps this disturbing detail that had the effect of

130

checking my dagger . . . What dagger? Don't make me laugh! I've never carried a weapon. Or was it fear that kept my hands from closing for ever round that slim throat? But fear of what?

Strangling! What am I talking about? Why not impalement with my iron-tipped walking-stick? I have already forgotten where I am coming from and what is hunting me or has marked me down; I cannot even remember how long I have been walking. One after another the heavy, silent pelicans flying along just above the water, all moving in a straight line in the same direction as myself, have passed me without turning their heads, their long necks bent back in the shape of an S. I am so tired now, exhausted by this interminable trek through sand that gives way beneath the soles of my shoes, that without realizing it I have started limping again. And when at last I reach the firm promenade, which has been ballasted, rolled, and asphalted for automobiles to drive and park on, I have to lean heavily on my silver-topped walking-stick to complete the last three hundred metres to the terrace of the Café Maximilian, where I sit down in my customary place. Pursued? But by whom? And for what reason?

The ball-players are there, as they are every morning. They are constantly on the move, and so suddenly and unpredictably that it is almost impossible to check their numbers in order to make sure that none of the girls is missing today, exceptionally. The few drinkers are fully occupied in reading their newspapers and the brown-haired student of the apricot-coloured complexion, sitting two metres from me, in writing, with repeated resumptions, some college essay or thesis on the ruled pages of the fat notebook covered with black canvas that she is holding open on her upraised knees, her bare feet with their vermilion-painted toenails resting on the next wicker chair along. And here comes the white-coated waiter with the strong Portuguese accent, walking towards my table in his nonchalant way to ask me what I want. All is in order.

I have had the first edition of *The Globe*, which had just arrived, brought to me at the same time as my white coffee and brioches. Almost the entire front page is given over, with enormous photos and banner headlines, to the mysterious murder of David G., the society dress-designer who was recently elevated to the peerage. My attention is immediately caught and held by a support article telling of a tragic episode that goes back to the adolescent years of his still very young wife, Lady Caroline: the suicide of the banker George de Saxe, father of the latter, the sole reason for which had been—according to the paper—a kidnap and ransom affair made up by the girl herself, the supposed victim of it, in aid of a terrorist organization. The banker, fearing the worst, apparently paid the incredible sum demanded, but at the cost of an operation that subsequently ruined his credit. Hearing then, in consequence of some error of communication that was never accounted for, of the execution of the prisoner by her abductors, he took his own life without waiting any longer.

Moreover other stories circulated about the father's disturbed relationship with his daughter as well as about the latter's astonishing resemblance to her own mother, who had disappeared at some time in the past in a ghastly accident, the circumstances of which were, again, never satisfactorily explained. It was this death that the girl had apparently wished to avenge. The article is headed: The New Atridae. The most surprising aspect of all this is undoubtedly the tranquil assurance with which so respectable a daily carries these utterly scandalous rumours concerning a family that, only a matter of days ago, appeared in high favour in the most official milieux of power and infuence.

At this precise point in my reflections, however, leafing through the remaining pages somewhat at random, I come across the photograph taken ostensibly by a reporter in an abandoned cannery and representing, so the caption says, the latest find made by the police in the ritual-sacrifices affair: the tortured body of an exception-ally beautiful adolescent girl, exhibited with arms chained behind her back and legs quartered on a machine designed for quite another purpose.

It is in this attitude, as I said, that Dr. Morgan finds her when he enters the cell where he does his work. He sits down by the bed, on the white-painted chair made of turned wood. He is tired after his long, harassing walk. After an indeterminate period during which he remains plunged in a kind of absence, or lethargy, he goes over and washes his hands carefully in the regulation enamelled basin; and he takes the opportunity of splashing a little water on his face. Then he commences the prescribed sequence of operations.

He first takes the usual measurements with regard to cardiac rhythm and respiration, applying his chromium-plated instruments to various points on the left breast, which he caresses mechanically in the process. Having established that all is in order, as I have already indicated, he administers the subcutaneous softening-up injection, the so-called total-availability shot, directly into the plump, firm flesh of the pubic pad. Finally, and very gently, he inserts a programmed ovule in the patient's vagina; this, it will be remembered, is a smooth white globe, the shape, appearance, and consistency of which are exactly those of a hard-boiled egg, shelled, from a small chicken. When the object has been completely sucked in and the orifice has almost closed up again, Morgan looks at the exact time on the large, old-fashioned gold watch he has taken from his waistcoat pocket.

Then he waits, from time to time consulting the table of mean durations and the indications of the stop-watch. When the time comes he checks the subject's reactions by means of short scratches, some deeper than others, executed with the point of a scalpel in the lower groin, on the insides of the thighs, and in the blond fleece around the vulva; the responses, gauged by looking at the eyes, which remain very mobile, the half-open mouth, and the whole body, which is free to express itself in various contortions or quivers, pass within the normal times from sharp pain to mild discomfort, and soon to quiet pleasure. Things are going to move fast now. The humiliation-method interrogation is scarcely finished before Angelica von Salomon embarks on her second narrative.

She is in the brightly-lit main foyer of the Opera House on the evening of a special performance. It is the interval. She wants to go to the lavatory, but she is experiencing very great difficulty in negotiating a passage through this throng of black suits and pale-coloured dresses blocking every possible exit with little groups that are both compact and in constant motion. Finding herself at last, without understanding why, in a less well lit but also very much less crowded gallery, she is struck by the presence, in these splendid surroundings, of a child virtually in rags who is attempting to sell her rosebuds to preoccupied gentlemen whose elegant hands, without their seeing her, push her away as one drives off smoke.

Having discovered the ladies' lavatory, more or less by chance, she tries to shut herself in one of the cubicles, but the lock does not work and she has to devise an uncomfortable stratagem in order somehow or other to block the heavy door with the judas in it . . . or rather with no judas . . . She becomes aware at this point that she must have forgotten, while dressing, to put on any panties, her routine no doubt disturbed by the particular care she was today devoting to her preparations: make-up, perfume, hair-do, etc. When she emerges she is terrified to see that the corridors, lobbies, and staircases are now quite deserted. She starts to run, alone and frail among the mirrors, marble statues, and columns, in order to regain her seat as quickly as possible.

Her father has taken a whole box for this intimate celebration of his beloved daughter Carolina's seventeenth birthday. She re-enters the box, rosy-cheeked, but no smile of welcome crosses the stern face: probably he wishes to punish her for being late. With the same gesture as he uses to make his dogs lie down he motions her towards the red-velvet seats, and she is surprised by the way in which they are arranged, which has changed in her absence: the two armless chairs in the front row on which they sat side by side for the preceding acts have been turned round, in other words they now have their short backs to the arm-rest at the front of the box.

In his habitually overbearing manner her father announces that this will give her a better view of the performance, with one knee on each seat. But the chairs have been placed unnecessarily far apart, and Caroline is about to protest when all at once the lights go out. She obeys in silence rather than start an argument, which she would find distressing and which might attract the attention of the neighbouring boxes, and is consequently obliged to spread her knees quite wide beneath the very full, flounced skirt of her long dress, having first lifted this up at the front in order at all events to avoid creasing the material. And she rests her two folded forearms on the stuffing with its covering of rough velvet lining the top of the balustrade. She has a better view of the stage as a whole, obviously, but she considers the position offensive and fit only for a little girl.

Her father has placed himself right behind her, standing between the two chairs; in fact this is probably the reason why he did not put them closer together: the present arrangement allows him to move right up against her and to see comfortably over her head. Her attention held by the new set—the wild rocks, the red-brown heath, and the sea below, smashing against the foot of the cliff—then by the shepherd's modulated lament, later blending with the song of hope and despair sung by Tristan as he lies dying of his wound, caught up immediately in the immemorial wait just beginning, Carolina does not immediately feel too clearly what is happening behind her back. In point of fact her father's right hand has slid beneath the ample skirt right up to the bare hip, subsequently descending towards the pit of the stomach. She attempts to repel this untimely contact as it becomes more explicit, she shifts slightly, makes one of the chairs squeak, half-turns the upper part of her body to murmur: Leave me alone . . .

But at this people start making urgent cries of *hush* all

136

around her; since her father, far from removing his hand, has on the contrary pressed himself shamelessly against her buttocks in order to caress her in greater comfort, and since she cannot even close her thighs, she decides to submit without saying anything . . . The wound . . . the ship . . . the waiting . . . The insidious fingers are no longer satisfied with stroking the pale-brown algae's silken tresses and the cleft—already moist, it would seem—between the polished walls of the marble cliffs. They pass back and forth in wave after wave, tirelessly, over the bivalvular lips, now slightly parted. The rising tide enters every little nook and cranny, parts the lacy fronds of a sea anemone, the water plunging and withdrawing in a continuous to-and-fro movement. The wound . . . the wound . . . One tiny, fragile rock resists and stiffens, buffeted by eddies and spume; yet it threatens, if this goes on, to shatter beneath too violent an impact. The ship . . . the ship . . . Carolina hasn't the strength left to hold back any longer from the pleasure that now fills her and at times swamps her. Before letting herself go completely she makes one final effort to open her eyes once more on the world of the living: the opulence of her surroundings, the presence in the half-darkness of a large and glittering audience, fear of the scandal, the impossibility of altering this pose in which she has been placed, all merge with the emotion rising from the orchestra in long, rolling waves that break one after another . . . Isolde's death aria plunges her into an ecstacy that goes on and on . . .

Abruptly, all the lights have come on again. Carolina, whose head was rolling on her arms as they grasped the rail, raises it as if she has just woken with a start. Is the last act over already, then? Or has she, by some over-obtrusive departure from accepted conduct, just interrupted the performance herself? Did they perhaps hear her moan with the flow beneath the singer's fortissimo passages? Two peremptory hands stand her up without a word. A large pool is spreading over the carpeted floor of the box between the chairs that have their backs to the balustrade. What liquid is this? What has been happening to her? She dare not look at her father. Having ventured a surreptitious glance, however, she cannot understand why tears are running down his cheeks, which it does not even occur to him to wipe away.

And why have the members of the audience risen to their feet without applauding? She lets herself be swept towards the exit, walking as if in her sleep in the middle of the jostling throng. There is an even more unusual commotion at the foot of the great staircase. Shouts and commands can be heard. Five or six helmeted policemen with rifles slung are trying to keep the inquisitive back from an area they have cleared. Someone says to her father in passing: There's been a murder.

Back home, she doesn't know why, in her all-white room, she immediately falls asleep with exhaustion. She is walking along a long, bare corridor, devoid of doors or any other openings but which turns abruptly at right angles for no visible reason, either to right or left, a great many times and in a wholly irregular fashion. At the same time, with each change of direction the passage becomes a little narrower. Nevertheless, there's no turning back. Don't ask questions, don't stop, don't look behind. For no visible reason, no reason.

She recognizes the place now: the convent of the kind sisters. She is fifteen. Her name is Christine. It is the much dreaded day of her first communion. She is in the chapel, kneeling on a red-and-black prie-dieu, flanked by six other girls apparently much younger than herself.

All seven are dressed in white veils—tulle, transparent embroidery, and lace—and crowned with spotless flowers such as one sees on Christian martyrs in picture-books. In a row facing the communicants as they wait for the host with hands together and mouths half open are twelve lighted candles, tall and slim and mounted on twelve silver candlesticks. Right at the back stands the altar, dominated by a cross of unpolished ebony measuring nearly three metres, with no figure, destined for the torture of the virgin; this is flanked by two more modest crosses of Baroque inspiration on which have been carved, in contorted poses, the nude figures of Violet and Lauretta, the two little whores crucified by way of a prelude on the same festive occasion.

Christine no longer knows quite what circumstances led to her completing the ceremony of religious initiation so late. A different and more distressing delay is very much more on her mind: since the end of the last lunar cycle, each passing day has convinced her a little more that that nocturnal visitation from the archangel in her cell, on her wrought-iron bed, cannot have been a dream. Taking her eyes off the cross that stands threateningly over her to lower them towards the region of her body that has just been pierced once again by that disturbing pain, very fierce yet gone in a flash, a lightning pain like a sword-thrust or the deep prick of a needle, Christine discovers to her horror that her white dress is now stained, in the region of the lower belly, by a small vermilion spot that is spreading with alarming rapidity, seeping into and, not encountering the least resistance, soaking through the various layers of light, porous material with which she is clad. Soon the whole central portion of her virginal costume is a single, blood-drenched disc, reminiscent of the Aunt Sally sideshow

139

glimpsed at a fair where the bride's veil went red when a shot found the middle.

But this is not the smacking of bullets into sheet-metal targets, nor the dull reports of automatic rifles; this sound is that of the drum rolls announcing the execution. Looming up suddenly before the altar, standing there motionless, the priest stares at the condemned girl with eyes slightly narrowed behind his steel-rimmed spectacles, which glitter with innumerable unbearably bright points of light. Christine would like to cry out, but no sound comes from her mouth. A cruel smile now contracts the priest's thin lips. And here, sure enough, are the iron-helmeted Roman soldiers who a moment ago were on guard at the foot of the great staircase, appearing suddenly behind her and seizing her with brutal, obscene gestures; there are three of them, and their big hands clamp down on her neck, her throat, her hips, pulling great fistfuls of the flimsy material in all directions, ripping and tearing away everything that falls beneath their fingers, holding up the bloody rags with hideous laughs and incomprehensible exclamations in a barbarous-sounding language. Before long all she has left to cover her nakedness is her mass of black hair, which has spread in thick, glossy curls over her shoulders and one breast. Mockingly the soldiers replace on her head the wreath that earlier fell to the floor: the white, sacrificial roses. And it takes them no more than a minute to nail the girl to the ebony cross, her arms stretched out sideways, a crude iron horseshoe nail driven into the hollow of each palm, the feet together and punched through in the same way with blows of the hammer, supported by a projecting bit of wood that forms a lip a metre from the ground.

Facing her now, the six little blond communicants have not moved. Moreover Christine, looking down from her cross, can now see that their hands, ostensibly joined in prayer, are in fact chained together to the arm-rests of their prie-dieus with iron rosaries, of which strong links constitute the beads. Undoubtedly terrified and not knowing what their turn will bring, they carefully hold their poses; and none of them flinches when the priest approaches their docile line and looks them in the eyes one by one as if trying to discover some guilty secret in the depths of pupils enlarged by the drug contained in the incense fumes.

He has picked up the first candle in passing, leaving the spike of the candlestick exposed, and he leans towards the faces at the risk of setting fire to the veils that form haloes around them, bringing the burning wick as close as possible, so that its slender, dancing redness is reflected in the mirror of each iris. Having inspected the little girls' twelve blue eyes in this fashion, the priest in his golden chasuble turns back to face the altar, holds the candle out at arm's length towards the tortured victim, whose strength is beginning to ebb, and in order to revive her extinguishes the flame by sinking it, between the tops of her thighs, several centimetres into the medial slit that lies open beneath the black triangle of fleece, now stained with vermilion. The young woman writhes feebly on her cross.

But the priest resumes the same business with the second candle, first using its light to scan the guilty reactions of the little girls still kneeling in the same position like statues of saints, then dousing the burning wick and its molten wax in the vagina of the crucified girl, who moves her body a little more with each fresh burn, writhing with hips and waist, opening her mouth inordinately wide, and making her swirling hair fling to right and left, since only her flower-wreathed head has

141

been left any scope for movement. As the seventh flame penetrates her, the spasm is so violent that she thinks she is dying . . .

Christine wakes up, shaken by an extended orgasm, on her iron bed. She has just had another visit from the archangel. All around, the room is bathed in reddish light. The girl nows sees quite clearly that she is not lying in her usual little bed with the wrought-iron spirals but in a heavy coffin of carved mahogany, the lid of which, decorated with a tall, massive cross, stands not far away against one of the marble columns of the mortuary chapel. Her father, wrapped in a black cloak for his solitary vigil, has fallen asleep in his chair beside her. Naked and adorned, Christine is lying on a bed of roses, flanked by twelve candles; only five of these, however, are still alight: the others have probably been blown out by draughts. One of them, near her feet, having toppled from its silver candlestick, has in falling set fire to the artificial flowers of silky gauze amongst which the girl has been laid out, arms slightly away from her sides and legs apart, like a doll in the flesh.

The flames spread rapidly, by degrees, up the groove between the thighs to the pubis, which catches fire in turn . . . Christine wants to shout, struggle . . . But the erl-king, who holds her firmly prisoner in invisible bonds, prevents her from even batting an eyelid and thus spoiling, if only for an instant, the still beauty of her face and her whole body. It is by moving her lips in an imperceptible fashion that, before losing consciousness altogether, she manages to murmur simply, as if in tender reproach: Father, can't you see I'm burning?

Dr. Morgan abruptly raises his lowered head, the inclination of which was becoming more and more pronounced and which just now collapsed under its own weight; he had fallen asleep with exhaustion, sitting on his white-painted chair in the laboratory cell. He immediately ascertains to his surprise that Angelica von Salomon has disappeared: the skeletal iron bed beside him is empty. He experiences a sharp sense of irritation. They must have come and fetched the prisoner for a fresh interrogation; but Morgan considers they could have notified him at least a few hours in advance rather than interrupt his experimental research during the course of a textual progression by taking advantage of a momentary sleep on his part, perfectly excusable in view of the surfeit of work currently keeping him busy day and night.

What a shambles! he exclaims out loud, thinking of the prison administration. The inspectors are all half mad, if not murderers. Chief Commissioner Duchamp thinks of nothing but gratifying his sexual whims. As for the guards and intelligence or enforcement officers, on the pretext that they often find themselves obliged to play a double game they now operate in so off-hand a manner that all control over them has become impossible; indeed one increasingly has the impression that they are deliberately working for the terrorist organizations themselves, for the call-girl racket, and for the drug traffickers, their official duties being no more than a convenient cover-up. Finally, certain highly-placed suspects take advantage of their social contacts to escape any kind of serious investigation conducted with appropriate and effective modern methods.

It seems obvious, for example, that the very young Lady G. ought to have been arrested there and then after the crime that cost her husband, Lord David, his life. In fact it would have been better to begin questioning her seriously prior to the deed; this might then have been, if not avoided, which hardly made sense, at least exploited more intelligently. But Morgan had the utmost difficulty even in managing to secure the imprisonment of two minor figures in the secret sections of headquarters: little Violet d'Eu and her friend Laura B., known as Lauretta, aged fourteen and sixteen respectively, members of Lady Caroline's private household who were employed ostensibly as chambermaids but whose actual duties must have been of a very much more personal nature, judging by the disturbing evidence collected by Temple, a false under-age beggar-girl disguised as an itinerant flower-seller, and disclosed to the chief commissioner just before the booby-trap went off in the main foyer of the Opera House.

Moreover Morgan is soon going to find himself further confirmed in his suspicions regarding the highly ramified undercurrents of this affair since, no more than a few hours later, he hears from the mouth of the chief commissioner himself that G. Court has been completely destroyed by a violent fire, which will make it impossible now to pursue investigations that were being held in abeyance (on whose orders?) among the considerable mass of files, records, or documents of various sorts collected and placed under seal by the investigating authorities but left, for the time being, where they were. The fire apparently started, by a curious coincidence, in a room built onto the vast house: the private chapel where the alleged Lord David lay in his sumptuous coffin, this

144

having been closed prematurely because of the appalling state in which the bomb had left the body, which was unrecognizable, blown into scattered fragments so that it was even hard to say whether there was a complete human being there or not, and of what age and which sex. The tall ceremonial candlesticks flanking him were to blame for the accident: a defective candle, deformed by the heat of its own combustion, had apparently overbalanced, collapsed on the artificial flowers of the funeral wreaths, and, in the absence of any surveillance, immediately set light to the red roses made of some synthetic material, celluloid-based and particularly inflammable—sometimes, depending on the circumstances, explosive.

The timber present in plenty from top to bottom of the building (the furniture, the old-style parquet flooring, the ceilings with no thermal insulation, the panelling, and even the carcasing of the walls) subsequently enabled the fire to spread with incredible speed through every part of the edifice, which for all its stately appearance was constructed entirely in lightweight materials, as was common practice at the time. The firemen, after a long struggle, managed only to inundate with great streams of water a few charred remains forming a paltry heap, as if all that had burned here had been a very small shed. But the most surprising thing is still the total disintegration of the coffin and its contents, so that none of the meticulous searches conducted without delay in the warm ashes, now packed into a crumbly or muddy paste, came up with the least vestige of it, the vaguest trace, in spite of its solid bronze mounts and the thick lead lining to which the funeral directors' representative drew attention. Everything seems to have volatilized in the furnace.

The first thing to catch my eye when I finally arrive on the scene by way of the avenue towards which only yesterday the flight of probably false pink-granite steps still descended is the fact that the very steps of this ostensibly stone staircase are no longer visible, nor is there anything left of the dense clumps of shrubbery that stood to either side of it. The entire mansion, which was to all appearances without a cellar, and its tiny garden are now reduced to a square of blackish mud, its surface broken by a few shapeless piles of dying embers from which the last wisps of smoke rise here and there, a quadrilateral the dimensions of which astonish by their smallness: it is hard to understand that there once stood on this site a splendid residence in which two dozen persons at least, masters and servants, dwelt in the greatest comfort.

That is not the end of the surprises, because there now appears, beyond this minute space cleared by the fire, the sloping street with the homely charm of centuries gone by, motionless and as if forgotten by time, that I came across on one of my extended Sunday strolls. And again it is that ageless tranquillity that strikes me. Motionless, I said, and that probably is the feeling still paramount today as one slowly climbs the pavement, the variable slope of which is so steep in places that two or three steps cut at an angle are necessary to restore a horizontal surface in front of each door.

It is already spring, the southern spring, and a pale, late-afternoon sun catches the first foliage, soft-green and beige, of the chestnuts, whose buds have just burst. The air is mild, all sounds far-off. There is no one in sight. The two-storeyed Directoire-style houses with their regular façades take on a pinkish tinge in the golden light, while through an open window the tinkling notes of a piano can be heard, the keys barely moving beneath the unenthusiastic fingers of a drowsy girl.

My nostalgic thoughts are suddenly interrupted when three people burst into view in front of me, coming out of an adjoining alley about twenty metres away and crossing the road at an angle with the slope; they are walking with evident haste, even a certain precipitation, towards the building that is exactly level with me on the other side of the street. I have just time, by starting back with a reflex movement towards the housefronts, to take cover behind a projecting staircase and its balustrade and to stoop down there, squeezing myself as far as possible into the corner. I am lucky to have been in this precise spot because such hiding-places—or even more scanty ones—are very scarce in this vicinity.

Fortunately the two men in raincoats and trilby hats seem to have little leisure to inspect their surroundings with any care, preoccupied as they are with holding up, or pulling along, or restraining a girl whom they flank securely; she is remarkable for her fair hair with its flame-coloured highlights (is this simply the effect of the setting sun backlighting the flowing curls?), and her elegance and glossy prettiness are sure indication of some such calling as cover-girl or film starlet. Her face, which is that of a disobedient doll, appears when for a moment it is turned towards me to be in the grip of the hazy effects of some narcotic drug.

It becomes quite obvious that her companions are conducting her by force to some unthinkable destination when, having inadvertently caught the heel of one of her delicate pale-blue shoes in the perforated cast-iron grating around a tree, onto which it is highly unlikely that she would have ventured of her own free will, she is literally dragged off it by her abductors with such brutality that she loses her shoe, which remains stuck in a hole in the grating, and has then to continue on her way hobbling on the toe of one black silk-stockinged foot, albeit for a very short distance: hardly have I had time to recognize to my great amazement that one of the men, whose face, half-hidden by his hat-brim, happens to be turned towards me, is none other than Inspector Victor Francis in person before the trio crosses the threshold formed by three stone steps that are cut off at an angle by the slope and disappears from view through an embrasure, the door having opened at their approach as if of its own accord, no doubt activated by some electronic device.

As soon as he is inside, feeling that he is out of sight at last, the false Inspector Francis leans back against the heavy steel door that has just closed behind him, the powerful machinery having as always made no sound during its four or five seconds' rotation but that sort of deep murmur one would think came from some nocturnal bird, never seen. Once his eyes have become somewhat accustomed to the bluish darkness filling the entrance of the tunnel that leads through the series of cells, chambers, or chapels with their multiple systems of complicated and baffling passages to the temple proper, Francisco Franco (this is the inspector's real name) sees, standing against the left wall apparently all ready for dispatch, the heavy cabin trunk with corners reinforced with heavy brass fittings and, at each end, the usual strong handle made of the same shiny yellow metal.

Shut in this trunk, according to what will be established later, bound hand and foot, carefully drugged for the duration of the journey only and breathing as best she can with the aid of intermittent puffs from a tranquillizing oxygen cartridge, is Marie-Ange Salome, proof of whose sanguinary, vampiric activities came out at her trial; for nine months she was engaged to Lord Corynth, whose strength was seen to decline progressively throughout

148

that period while the two little red marks at the base of his neck became more pronounced from week to week, marks that the family physician, the famous Dr. Morgan . . .

Could you, the interrogator's neutral voice interrupts, now make the requisite quick chronological résumé, accurate and complete but without getting bogged down in unnecessary detail, of all the events that took place from the morning of this important day? It is a very simple matter for me to satisfy this after all quite natural request, so I begin without further urging.

7 a.m. Sunrise. The narrator searches the ins and outs of his recent memory for a vanishing recollection. He has the impression he is losing ground.

7.12 a.m. On a beach near the town centre some civil guards kill, by mistake, little Temple, a thirteen-year-old equestrienne who displays her perverted talents at the Michelet Circus every evening and spends the rest of the night working in a private capacity for the chief commissioner of police.

7.24 a.m. The narrator, wishing to build his defence on solid foundations, sets out to describe his cell.

7.36 a.m. Late arrival of the fire engines at the scene of an accident reported in an anonymous phone call. Fire completely ravages a luxurious private house dating from the early years of the century, at any rate situated in a very ancient quarter, the demolition of which has already been negotiated between the council and a property-development group.

7.48 a.m. Encounter, down by the shore, with an alleged beggar-girl dragging a lion (or aurochs?) skin across the sand. In fact, as will soon become apparent, this is Marie-Ange, twin sister of Angelica von Salomon, from whom she is indistinguishable, apart from a get-up that

149

can scarcely escape attention, except by the unvarying complexion of the pale redhead, her milk-white skin refusing to tan despite a life lived often in the open air.

8 a.m. A patrol picks out from various pieces of jetsam deposited by the high tide right at the top of the beach several false beer-cans that evidently once contained white powder.

8.12 a.m. The chief commissioner of police, alerted immediately, gives orders for Dr. Morgan to be arrested. This decision is never in fact put into execution.

8.24 a.m. Lady Caroline wakes up. The young woman attempts to recount to her favourite slave an erotic nightmare that made her yell out loud in the middle of the night. She will discover yet again, to her cost, that dreams should be noted down on the instant, which would not have been difficult for her to do since for a good hour she remained tossing and turning in her too-warm bed before getting off to sleep again.

From 8.36 to 8.48 a.m. the narrator tries to make a slip-knot (to hang himself) with his wire coat-hanger. He does not succeed, the metal being too stiff.

9 a.m. An explosion of criminal origin destroys most of the factory that used to manufacture dubious tinned salmon as well as the whole neighbourhood for a long way back. The hydropathic itself is badly damaged.

From 9.12 to 9.24 a.m., capture (doomed subsequently to failure, as we know) of Vanessa, the student decoy, on the terrace of the Café Maximilian.

9.36 a.m. Discovery of the shoe with the mirror, wedged by the heel in a chestnut-tree grating not far from the Gainsboro residence. The investigation immediately takes on a fresh dimension.

9.48 a.m. The narrator recovers consciousness following a short black-out that he attributes to lack of food.

10. a.m. A cayman farm is devastated by fire. The giant reptiles escape. They will completely overrun the city's entire network of sewers.

10.12 a.m. The investigating officers take a faked photograph, in the ruins of the salmon factory, of the more than half-naked body of a pretty welding operative who has in fact been missing for several weeks, if not longer. However, there is every indication that she was in no way a victim of the deflagration. Questionable intervention on the part of the narrator.

10.24 a.m. Marie-Ange Salome enters the church in a gorgeous white dress, the translucent, filmy attire of the traditional bride. She is resplendently beautiful. Lord Corynth, on the other hand, her husband-to-be, appears to be more and more seriously affected by the strange decline that has kept him a recluse for the past few months. He is said to have wanted to bring forward the wedding ceremony, which was originally to have taken place at the beginning of May, for fear he might die of exhaustion before the happy day.

From 10.36 to 10.48 a.m. little Violetta, who on the pretext that she is ill is enjoying a lie-in after breakfasting in bed, leafs through an illustrated children's book recounting exciting episodes from ancient history. The child surreptitiously begins caressing herself under the sheets.

11 a.m. The fair Angelique arrives on the beach in front of the Café Rudolph, clutching her pink-and-white beach-ball under her left arm and a green apple in her right hand. The narrator opens the black notebook to jot this down, or perhaps merely to check a detail of this entrance written down earlier. First gust of over-warm wind heralding the brief tornado that is going to spread panic among the bathers.

11.12 a.m. The narrator looks at himself in the greenish, broken mirror fixed to the wall of his cell.

11.24 a.m. Lord Gainsboro receives an invitation card for a very special kind of hunt.

11.36 a.m. Franck V. Francis reaches the mouth of the tunnel, switches on his torch, and embarks on a tricky exploration. A steady, crystalline dripping sound (is it water?) punctuates the silence, revealing the existence of underground cisterns.

11.48 a.m. The coffin of Count David de G. is recovered, empty, on a piece of waste ground.

12.00 noon. Chief Commissioner Duchamp has himself served a delicious meal by Angelica von Salomon, in the nude apart from the chains binding her hands behind her back. (The original version of the report had, in place of these last few phrases, the words "in an outfit at once simple and intricate".) Brief description of the premises. Arching, contorsions of various kinds, and awkward postures necessitated by the prisoner's bonds (recommended to the chief commissioner by two interrogation warders). The lovely Angelique, condemned to death by quartering, is to be executed the following day; Duchamp, faithful to one of his favourite customs, has ordered that she be delivered over to him beforehand in order that he may spend the afternoon and then the whole night with her, deriving, as he says, great refreshment from sleeping in the warmth of a victim already destined for the executioners' instruments. During lunch the girl will be punished for her inevitable clumsiness by various preliminary tortures involving a greater or lesser degree of burning or blood-letting but not permanently impairing the outward appearance of her body.

12.12 p.m. The stone falling.

12.24 p.m. Marie-Ange Salome enters the Church of

the Holy Spirit in the dazzling, virgin-white costume of the traditional bride, etc.

12.36 p.m. At the Morgan Clinic, Lady Caroline enters her friend Angelique's monastic room. This is the first time she has been to see her since her accident. The girl, it will be remembered, very nearly drowned out towards the end of the wharf in somewhat confused circumstances. Dressed in a fetching pink nuisette, she is at the moment lying on her bed, propped up on the many pillows that are piled against the spirals and ogee arches of the elaborate wrought-iron bedhead. Caroline is struck by the rapid disappearance from the convalescent's face of the golden-brown colour gained not long since in the bright sunshine. In her new pallor Angelica appears to have even larger eyes, these being no doubt also accentuated by rings like those that pleasure produces. She lies motionless, greeting her mistress's appearance with no more than the vaguest smile of welcome. Resting on her outstretched thighs is a white plate on which there are three soft-boiled eggs, shelled but still intact. Slowly she reaches out a thin, tapering hand to begin, without appetite, her insipid midday snack. At this point Caroline notices red lines ringing each of her wrists; seized with an inexplicable fear, she tries to check the invalid's gesture. Angelique, however, believing that she is being reprimanded for eating with her fingers, starts to laugh in an odd, exaggerated manner—like a madwoman, Lady Caroline thinks.

12.48 p.m. The director of the Opera House receives orders to replace *Tristan* by *The Firebird* for the official gala reopening.

1 p.m. Angelique gradually inserts a whole egg in her mouth without biting or squashing it, much to her visiting friend's alarm.

1.12 p.m. Marie-Ange Salome enters the Church of the Holy Spirit accompanied by the whole procession in ceremonial robes. Followed by the six little girls supporting her long train, she goes and kneels on the magnificent red-and-black prie-dieu that has been set up facing the altar. Lord Corynth, as pale as death, does the same on an identical seat beside her.

1.24 p.m. In the course of his circumspect progress underground Franck V. Francis discovers several rooms adjoining the main gallery, comprising a series of upright circular panels, standing about two metres high (almost touching the irregular vault carved out of the rock) and each bearing seven concentric circles drawn in red paint, which look to him like targets for shooting practice. From the floor of beaten earth he picks up a large quantity of artificial pearls, remarkable for their size and perfection.

1.36 p.m. Arrival of Dr. Morgan in the experimentation chamber. He sits down at the patient's bedside. The ninth narrative is already in progress.

1.48 p.m. Kidnap of Marie-Ange from the Church of the Holy Spirit. As if this were the prearranged signal, the sudden appearance of the hired ruffians before the altar follows immediately upon the priest's gesture in inserting the host in the still half-open mouth of the young bride, who is very much afraid of biting the flesh of the god if she brings her teeth too close together. Her small, neatly ranged, perfectly regular incisors and her canines, as sharp as if they had been honed like awls, gleam dazzlingly white between her full lips, which look as if they have been freshly licked to make them shine more, and the tiny tip of an even moister tongue. The victim dare not even cry out during the abduction for fear of tearing the sacrament. Those present are petrified, none of them

154

moving a muscle, all holding their breath in excitement at the miracle that is taking place. Lord Corynth faints, his body sinking to the granite flags with a thud.

2 a.m. Descending to the depths of the crypt of the ancient Gothic building, dragging their prey behind them, the abductors check that the latter's Titian-red pubis is indeed, as the report mentions, incrusted with nine black diamonds. The narrator puzzles over the meaning of this sentence, which cannot be a simple metaphor.

2.12 p.m. Again the stone falling, motionless.

2.24 p.m. The heavy trunk with the brass corners is loaded onto a funeral ferryman's mortuary bark that was waiting at the little postern closing off the end of the tunnel. The height at which this opening is situated in the sheer face of the cliff on which the cathedral stands has always suggested that it was used solely for throwing witches into the river, some more alive than others after being put through a lengthy confession of their imaginary misdeeds, as recorded in the bill of indictment, with the aid of suitable tortures, an exhaustive inventory of which fills the twelve registers of the great codex. This spring, however, the flood level is so high that the water now washes the bottom of the three steps hacked out of the hard rock here and polished by bare feet.

2.36 p.m. Lady Gainsboro, returning home, inadvertently reads the invitation to the rather special hunt and suddenly realizes (as, in point of fact, she was beginning to suspect) that her young husband, far from being a homosexual as he lets people think, is a member of the Society of the Golden Triangle. On the other hand she knows already that the temple can no longer be kept supplied with fresh inmates, as it was at the outset, by captures made in the course of the regular mopping-up operations carried out in the districts infested with gangs of youths living wild, only the boys being on those occasions massacred systematically during or after the fighting. Carolina, whose apprehensions have been on the increase ever since she left the clinic, is now concerned for Lord David's very life. She decides nevertheless to keep the date with her lover in the bathing-hut right at the end of the beach.

2.48 p.m. Inspector Francis's electric torch all of a sudden goes out. Unable to relight it, he throws it away at random in the darkness that envelops him like a shroud, halting his slow progress through the tunnel at the very moment when he was at last nearing the end.

3 p.m. Appearance, yet again, on the presentation wall of the cell, still in the same silence with its crystalline dripping, of the ghost of Marie-Ange Salome. She is naked except for the arabesques of pearls or diamonds that here and there adorn her goddess-like body. In her left hand she holds the fleece of the slain lion, its heavy, red-brown folds trailing on the ground behind her. The magic violin in her right hand gleams like a dangerous present. Her green eyes, huge and staring, are fixed on the narrator.

3.12 p.m. The big pelicans fly past, skimming the water, motionless.

3.24 p.m. The police burst into the photographic laboratory with the secret exit where E. Manroy is busy operating. Although Angelica von Salomon was taken away several hours ago, the two men easily recognize this innocent special-effects enthusiast as the Dr. William Morgan whose disconnected trail they have been following since the morning. The latter had reached that point in the account of the crime where the bride with the over-intimate jewellery, tied to a target in the position of a

St. Andrew's cross, is being diced for by the marksmen who, one by one, now turn their astonished faces towards the intruders, and are still.

3.36 p.m. Again the stone falling.

Motionless, as I said, alone, with the only sound from now on, off and on, that of water dripping to no purpose in a space that has become even smaller, as I was saying . . . What did I say? What did I do?

Selected Grove Press Paperbacks

62480-7 ACKER, KATHY / Great Expectations: A Novel / $6.95

17458-5 ALLEN, DONALD & BUTTERICK, GEORGE F., eds. / The Postmoderns: The New American Poetry Revised / $9.95

17397-X ANONYMOUS / My Secret Life / $4.95

62433-5 BARASH, D. and LIPTON, J. / Stop Nuclear War! A Handbook / $7.95

17087-3 BARNES, JOHN / Evita—First Lady: A Biography of Eva Peron / $4.95

17208-6 BECKETT, SAMUEL / Endgame / $3.50

17299-X BECKETT, SAMUEL / Three Novels: Molloy, Malone Dies and The Unnamable / $6.95

17204-3 BECKETT, SAMUEL / Waiting for Godot / $3.95

62064-X BECKETT, SAMUEL / Worstward Ho / $5.95

17244-2 BORGES, JORGE LUIS / Ficciones / $6.95

17112-8 BRECHT, BERTOLT / Galileo / $3.95

17106-3 BRECHT, BERTOLT / Mother Courage and Her Children / $2.95

17393-7 BRETON ANDRE / Nadja / $6.95

17439-9 BULGAKOV, MIKHAIL / The Master and Margarita / $5.95

17108-X BURROUGHS, WILLIAM S. / Naked Lunch / $4.95

17749-5 BURROUGHS, WILLIAM S. / The Soft Machine, Nova Express, The Wild Boys: Three Novels / $5.95

62488-2 CLARK, AL, ed. / The Film Year Book 1984 / $12.95

17535-2 COWARD, NOEL / Three Plays (Private Lives, Hay Fever, Blithe Spirit) / $7.95

17219-1 CUMMINGS, E.E. / 100 Selected Poems / $3.95

17327-9 FANON, FRANZ / The Wretched of the Earth / $4.95

17483-6 FROMM, ERICH / The Forgotten Language / $6.95

17390-2 GENET, JEAN / The Maids and Deathwatch: Two Plays / $8.95

17838-6 GENET, JEAN / Querelle / $4.95

17662-6 GERVASI, TOM / Arsenal of Democracy II / $12.95

17956-0 GETTLEMAN, MARVIN, et.al. eds. / El Salvador: Central America in the New Cold War / $9.95

17648-0 GIRODIAS, MAURICE, ed. / The Olympia Reader / $5.95

62490-4 GUITAR PLAYER MAGAZINE / The Guitar Player Book (Revised and Updated Edition) $11.95

62003-8 HITLER, ADOLF / Hitler's Secret Book / $7.95

17125-X HOCHHUTH, ROLF / The Deputy / $7.95

62115-8 HOLMES, BURTON / The Olympian Games in Athens, 1896 / $6.95

17209-4 IONESCO, EUGENE / Four Plays (The Bald Soprano, The Lesson, The Chairs, and Jack or The Submission) / $6.95

17226-4 IONESCO, EUGENE / Rhinoceros / $5.95

62123-9 JOHNSON, CHARLES / Oxherding Tale / $6.95

17254-X KEENE, DONALD, ed. / Modern Japanese Literature / $12.50

17952-8 KEROUAC, JACK / The Subterraneans / $3.50

62424-6 LAWRENCE, D.H. / Lady Chatterley's Lover / $3.95

17016-4 MAMET, DAVID / American Buffalo / $4.95

17760-6 MILLER, HENRY / Tropic of Cancer / $4.95

17295-7 MILLER, HENRY / Tropic of Capricorn / $3.95

17869-6 NERUDA, PABLO / Five Decades: Poems 1925-1970. Bilingual ed. / $12.50

17092-X ODETS, CLIFFORD / Six Plays (Waiting for Lefty, Awake and Sing, Golden Boy, Rocket to the Moon, Till the Day I Die, Paradise Lost) / $7.95

17650-2 OE, KENZABURO / A Personal Matter / $6.95

17232-9 PINTER, HAROLD / The Birthday Party & The Room / $6.95

17251-5 PINTER, HAROLD / The Homecoming / $5.95

17539-5 POMERANCE, BERNARD / The Elephant Man / $5.95

17827-0 RAHULA, WALPOLA / What the Buddha Taught / $6.95

17658-8 REAGE, PAULINE / The Story of O, Part II; Return to the Chateau / $3.95

62169-7 RECHY, JOHN / City of Night / $4.50

62001-1 ROSSET, BARNEY and JORDAN, FRED, eds. / Evergreen Review No. 98 / $5.95

62498-X ROSSET, PETER and VANDERMEER, JOHN / The Nicaragua Reader / $9.95

17119-5 SADE, MARQUIS DE / The 120 Days of Sodom and Other Writings / $12.50

62009-7 SEGALL, J. PETER / Deduct This Book: How Not to Pay Taxes While Ronald Reagan is President / $6.95

17467-4 SELBY, HUBERT / Last Exit to Brooklyn / $3.95

17948-X SHAWN, WALLACE, and GREGORY, ANDRE / My Dinner with Andre / $6.95

17797-5 SNOW, EDGAR / Red Star Over China / $9.95

17260-4 STOPPARD, TOM / Rosencrantz and Guildenstern Are Dead / $3.95

17474-7 SUZUKI, D.T. / Introduction to Zen Buddhism / $3.95

17599-9 THELWELL, MICHAEL / The Harder They Come: A Novel about Jamaica / $7.95

17969-2 TOOLE, JOHN KENNEDY / A Confederacy of Dunces / $4.50

17418-6 WATTS, ALAN W. / The Spirit of Zen / $3.95

GROVE PRESS, INC., 196 West Houston St., New York, N.Y. 10014